THE BUTTERFLY'S STROKE
AND OTHER STORIES

ANNMARIE SANSEVERO

PUBLISHING

Stark Publishing
Waterloo, ON
www.starkpublishing.ca

The Butterfly's Stroke and Other Stories / Annmarie SanSevero
First paper printing September 2025

CONTENTS

To Martin L. Shoemaker

You are my mentor and friend. Not only are you a talented author and coder, you are also incredibly generous with your knowledge, and patient as I learn. I'm pretty sure I mumble "Tools not Rules" in my sleep.

Without you, not only would this collection not exist, but my life would not be the same. I'm blessed to have you as a part of my journey.

INTRODUCTION TO "THE BUTTERFLY'S STROKE"

Years ago, when I was in high school (don't ask how long ago that was), I read a story about Joni Erikson. Joni went swimming with some friends and dove into shallow water paralyzing her. That story stuck with me. Fast forward to my current age (you can't ask that either). I read about the Neuralink technology in development, a brain/computer interface. I started thinking what if we could use a wireless connection to link it to the spinal cord and enable limb movement. That was the seed that led to The Butterfly's Stroke.

1

THE BUTTERFLY'S STROKE

Nadia sat in her wheelchair holding a paintbrush in her mouth, her dark curly hair safely out of the way in a French braid. When she'd first started her new hobby, Nadia hated the smell of the acrylic paint which filled her bedroom; but like everything else in her new normal, she'd adjusted.

Her mother had been careful to place the easel as far as possible from her frilly white canopy bed. After all, being a quadriplegic was no excuse for a messy bedroom. Not that she was the one to clean it anymore. It's funny the things she didn't appreciate. What she wouldn't give to clean anything right now—even a toilet.

On the wall behind her canvas hung all her swim medals and memorabilia, including her Olympic team photo. Her mother offered to move it out of site, but Nadia didn't want to forget. She wanted to swim again. Really swim. Not just float lifeless in the water like a CPR dummy that someone dragged into the pool. She wanted to feel the water on her skin and strain her muscles with each stroke that propelled her toward the other end of the lane. She wanted her spot on the Olympic team again.

Today, painting was a merciful distraction. Just one more night and she'd be the first human to get a Butterfly. All her dreams were now pinned on something the size of a quarter. After the surgery, she'd either have control over her body once more or have all her hope destroyed.

Tilting her head forward, Nadia pressed a green blob of paint on her canvas. She hoped to turn it into a cheerful tree-top. Thus far, her paintings had yet to produce the shapes she could so clearly see in her head.

On her first attempt to paint, she couldn't go more than a few minutes before her mouth cramped, but she refused to give up. Besides, when you can't feel most of your body, even a cramp is interesting. Now she could paint for almost twenty minutes.

There was a soft knock on her bedroom door.

"Come in!" Nadia shouted as the paintbrush dropped from her mouth. "Shoot. Note to self, remember when mouth is already occupied."

Carrie was the one member of the swim team that still came to see her. Once it became apparent Nadia wouldn't be leaving the chair, the others slowly drifted away.

Almost a full head shorter than Nadia when she could stand, Carrie's 5'1'' body was a powerhouse in the water. She was one of the few people that could match Nadia's own stubborn tenacity to not be told what her body couldn't do.

Carrie walked in smiling, grabbed the paintbrush from Nadia's lap, and placed it in the nearby glass container. Her head tilted as she looked at the blob of green on the canvas. "An overweight Oscar the Grouch?"

"Shut up."

"What in the world made you decide to take up painting?" Carrie asked.

"My mother had me watch one of those 'inspirational' movies about some other teenager who became a quadriplegic from like 60 years ago. She had to learn how to write with her mouth and then took up painting. I figured if some ancient person from like the 1970s can do it, so can I."

"Fair enough."

"Are you here for funsies or as a last visit in case I die tomorrow?" Nadia asked.

"Eww," Carrie said. "You're not going to die in surgery. Why would you even say that?"

"It's my mom's secret fear," Nadia said.

"Not so secret if she told you."

"She wouldn't actually say that to me. I overheard her on the phone. Honestly, I think she's been afraid of something happening to me since dad died. Combine that with my accident and she pretty much lives in a constant state of fear."

"Well, moms are designed to worry. Tomorrow is about you, who, by the way, is going to come out of this surgery alive and able to move again," Carrie said.

"I'll give you alive, but Dr. Zhao keeps reminding me I'm the first to have this procedure and he's not making any promises. Like I didn't know what experimental meant. Dr. Dimples is lucky he's so cute." Nadia used her sip and puff device to turn the wheelchair toward Carrie.

"One of these days you're going to accidentally call him Dr. Dimples in person," Carrie said. "Oh! I saw your interview on the news last night. I didn't realize a robot was doing the surgery."

"Mr. Roboto is only doing the brain part, the implant and threads. The receptor in my spine is being done by a regular old human. Hey, maybe the electrodes on the threads will allow me to hack into things. I could become the first brain hacker."

"Dark."

Nadia's mother popped her head in. Before life fell apart, she could have passed for her older sister. Now, her face wore the agony of the last few years in deep lines and sunken eyes. "Nadia needs to get some rest. We have an early start tomorrow."

"Okay," Carrie said. "I'll come see you as soon as they let me."

She leaned down and kissed the top of Nadia's head.

THE ROOM slowly came into focus. She could see machines everywhere. Her head felt heavy. Groggy. She could feel that. What she couldn't feel was her body. It didn't work. No walking. No swimming. Not even the ability to feed herself. She tried to hold back the tears she'd be unable to wipe from her face.

"Good afternoon, Sleeping Beauty," a nurse said as she came to check Nadia's vitals.

"It didn't work," Nadia said. "I can't feel anything new. Does my mom know?"

"Now hold on," the nurse said. "They've implanted everything but haven't turned it on yet. Remember? Dr. Zhao didn't want to overwhelm your senses as you woke up from surgery."

The tears broke through. That's right. He'd told her that. She still had a chance. The nurse swiped a tissue from somewhere and gently wiped her cheeks.

"I'll get your mom and the docs," she said.

A few minutes later her mother walked in looking nervous, followed by her medical team, one neurosurgeon/computer guru, one orthopedic surgeon, and their nurse. They'd spent so much time together, they felt more like friends sometimes.

Dr. Kevin Zhao, AKA Dr. Dimples, was the brain/computer genius of the squad. One day she hoped to have a man look at her the way Dr. Dimples looked at brain scans and computer code.

"Should I leave you two alone?" Nadia said.

Kevin looked at her excitedly, "The surgery went perfect! Now let's make some magic. You ready?"

Nadia smiled. "I hope you're ready to run. I did promise to chase you down and make you buy me dinner."

"Ah!" Kevin said lifting up one of his legs. "I came prepared. I wore tennis shoes just in case you start that chase right away. I have to play hard to get, right?" His face turned serious. "We're going to turn on the connections a few at a time, starting with your arms. Tell me when you feel something."

Kevin tapped a few keys on the computer.

"I can feel something." Nadia almost shouted the words. "It feels like there are ants inside my arm." She looked over at her mom, who was already crying.

A cheer went up from the remainder of the team. "Good. Okay, I'm going to complete the electrodes for your arms and start your torso."

Nadia inhaled deeply, then a wide smile broke out across her face. "I can feel the sheets!" She laughed. Who would have thought that feeling bed sheets underneath you would be one of the best gifts ever? "Oh! I have an itch. My arm itches!"

She started blubbering. It felt amazing to have an itch on her arm. Her right arm moved over and awkwardly scratched.

Through watery eyes Nadia noticed she wasn't the only one in the room crying.

~

MONTHS OF GRUELING rehabilitation as Nadia retrained her muscles had finally paid off. Today wasn't one of her daily neural checks and tests. It was a performance. In front of a mass of news media she would swim the I.M. that got her on the Olympic team before the accident. Science was expensive and she was the big fundraiser. As long as it kept her swimming she didn't mind.

The parking lot had several vans from local news agencies. Her mother turned off the ignition for their silver Honda EV and started to open the door.

"How cool would it be if I went in there and broke my personal record?" Nadia said.

"Maybe lower your expectations a bit," her mom said. "There's still a delay in the receptors and your muscles are out of practice."

Nadia sighed. "I know. I know. You wouldn't want me to dream small, though, would you?"

Her mother smiled. "You've never done anything small. Just remember, you don't have to be an Olympian for me to be proud of you."

"I know," Nadia said as she squeezed her mother's hand.

"Good. Now go kick some I.M. tail."

As they walked in Nadia inhaled the chloramines in the air. She'd grown to love the smell of that contaminant. Groups of reporters huddled in little cliques. It was weird knowing she was the focus of those huddles. Her eyes shifted to the pool. The glassy surface of the placid water reflected the lights above. No one had put the lane dividers out. This was what happened when non-swimmers were put in charge.

"I'll get a lane set up for you," her mom said as she took off toward the storage reel. It was nice seeing her back in swim-mom mode.

"Nadia!" Kevin shouted from the other side of the room.

His voice echoed and suddenly she was being swarmed by reporters.

The questions flew at her.

"How are you feeling about swimming a medley again?"

"Will your team be here?"

"Do you think you'll ever swim competitively again?"

"What has been the hardest adjustment to your neural implant?"

Kevin pushed through the crowd. "Hold on. You'll all get a chance to ask your questions, but this is Nadia's moment. Plus, scientists have work to do."

He grabbed onto her arm and steered her away from the unsatisfied journalists toward the computer system they used to monitor her neural implant.

Most of the time they could transfer data wirelessly, but they also had a tiny interface just to the right of the part in her hair where they could manually access her brain. Dr. Dimples had backups for his backups.

She always felt like a cyborg in a movie when the computer line was attached to her head.

Once a month they used maintenance mode for a hard download and compared it to the wireless data. Those were the appointments she hated, because it meant shutting her implant down during the data transfer. There was always that horrific moment where she went from feeling everything to nothing, like those nightmares where you are running but your body won't move. Then she'd lie there trying not to panic about the possibility it wouldn't turn back on. After all, computers glitch, right?

Nurse Julie had once told her there was a kill switch that snipped the threads if things went berserko on her. After she'd learned it was unrecoverable, she warned each of the docs that she'd hire a hitman if any of them flipped that switch.

"It's time," Kevin said.

With the lane ready, Nadia slipped off her sweats and stepped onto the block. The butterfly was her worst stroke, but at least it would be over first. Her mother blew the horn and Nadia pushed off. The strain in her shoulders felt great. Pull, push, recover. The tightening in her abs during her dolphin kicks gave her a bit of a rush. This was home.

As she turned to do her backstroke, her right arm wouldn't move. She found herself going in a circle. Then her left arm gave out. Her heart began to race. She heard a splash behind her.

No way was she going to let herself be dragged from this pool. She stood up to see Dr. Dimples had jumped in, lab coat and all.

"Stop!" she yelled at him. "I've got this. It's just a cramp," she lied. "Now get out of my lane." She'd tell Dr. Dimples the truth later. First, she'd finish her medley.

"It's not a cramp," Kevin yelled. "The readings are all over the place. Let's get you out of the pool."

He dragged himself through the water toward her.

Nadia jumped up and down in the water to show Kevin she had control, while desperately trying to get her neural electrodes to communicate with her arms by sheer force of will.

"Trust me," she yelled at him. "I've got this."

She felt a sharp pain in her head. Her body flooded with a feeling of euphoria. Then, her arm twitched. A few seconds later, she could move them again. Relieved, she smiled and met Kevin's eyes.

"Trust me."

∼

THE MEDIA HAILED it as a success and dubbed her the "Spunky Swimmer." Kevin told them the crazy readings were from her brain adjusting to the new movements. While the media bought it, she could tell Kevin was worried.

NADIA FLOPPED onto her canopy bed. Her eyes drifted toward the easel which had been folded up in a corner since her procedure. She'd thought about trying to paint now that she had full mobility but doubted that was why her paintings were terrible.

Nadia.

Someone called her name. Weird, she thought it came from inside her room. Even weirder, she thought it was her voice.

"Mom, did you call me?" Nadia shouted from her bed.

Her bedroom door opened, and her mother popped her head in. "Did you call me, dear?"

"Yeah, I was wondering if you called my name."

Her mother shook her head. "Nope. Just watching T.V. Maybe that's what you heard."

"O.K., thanks."

Her mother re-closed the door and went back to her show. Maybe it was the T.V.

Nadia.

This time the voice was a little louder. It definitely came from her head. Was her implant misfiring? Her body tensed and she methodically lifted and moved each arm and leg one at a time just to make sure she still had control of her limbs. Everything worked fine. Maybe it was exhaustion. She'd get some sleep and see Kevin and the team tomorrow for a check.

NADIA WOKE WITH A START. She'd dreamt she was trapped in a gelatinous sac. She pushed and tried to tear at it but couldn't make any headway. Someone shouted her name. The room was dark, and she was still in her day clothes. Heart racing, Nadia rolled over and grabbed her phone. 2:43 am. At least there was more time to sleep. She pulled back the bed covers and curled up underneath them. A light flashed behind her eyes. Something was wrong. Maybe she should wake the team and go in now?

No, she'd just put her mother in a complete panic. Better if she acted like everything was fine. The team would figure it out.

NADIA ARRIVED at the lab early for her checkup. The neuroscience unit was painted a bland beige and off-white. You'd think a group determined to improve brain function would have put some effort into visually stimulating decor. This looked more like they shared a decorator with the state penitentiary.

Three nurses stood working behind the curved half wall that separated them from visitors. Two other employees were at a computer typing away. As she approached to check-in, a couple of them started clapping.

"Hi, Spunky Swimmer," said one of the nurses. "We caught you on the news. Can we get your autograph?"

"You're hysterical."

The nurse pushed the button to open the double doors which led to the lab.

Her home away from home was well lit. To the far left was the bed they used when she was in maintenance mode. She hated that bed. Next to that was a computer station. Against the center wall, all the recording equipment was carefully secured to the desks and shelving, along with some more computers. At the far end of the room was a table where she would eat or the team would go over results. Kevin was sitting at one of the desks staring at a brain map they took during her swim, completely absorbed as usual.

"I know my brain is sexy, but you shouldn't stare quite so hard," Nadia said when the double doors closed behind her.

Kevin jumped just a little at the sound of her voice. "I didn't even hear you come in." He pointed to the chair next to him. "Have a seat. I want to show you something."

Nadia never could see the brain maps exactly the way Kevin did, but sat down anyway. Mostly she just nodded and agreed with whatever he said she should be seeing.

"Do you see this area at the hypothalamus? The substantia nigra, ventral tegmental area?"

"Ummm....sure."

"That's where Dopamine is produced," he said. "You had an explosion of it at—"

"Explosion?" That sounded bad.

"Not literal. I mean a large amount was released after the readings went crazy. I want to do a visual scan."

When you spend enough time around doctors and scientists, you get to know their moods. This one scared her. "You sound worried."

"Not worried," Kevin said quickly. "Curious. Let's do a maintenance download."

Nadia groaned.

"I know," Kevin said. "But you have my awesome company."

He gave her one of his dimpled smiles, which she was starting to think he used to get his way a lot.

He picked up his phone and a minute later the rest of his team entered. Blaine, an Ivy League graduate who, even in scrubs, looked like old money with his Ken doll hair and vacation tan, always offered to help her onto the hospital bed.

"Thanks, Blaine. I kind of want to do it myself today."

Blaine smiled and stepped back, giving her space. "You got it."

Nadia lowered the side rail and hopped up onto the bed, dreading what was coming next. She stretched out on her back and Nurse Julie, with her mass of red hair pulled back in a bun, placed the cable in the port on her head, along with a blood pressure cuff and a pulse oximeter.

"Ready?" Kevin asked.

"No, but go ahead anyway."

She saw Kevin frown. She suspected he hated turning off her neural link almost as much as she did, but it was a procedural necessity.

Within a minute her body went numb. It happened a little at a time as they turned off the electrodes. It made her wonder if this is what dying felt like. Once the last electrode was off, Nadia worked to hold back the panic. She wasn't really trapped in her body again. This was temporary. It took about 20 minutes or so to download the data. Kevin stayed glued to his computer to read what he could as it came in.

"Blaine, come here," Kevin said.

Nadia turned her head but couldn't turn over to see more of what was going on. She heard Kevin pointing something out and their voices went lower.

"Hey!" Nadia said. "Anyone want to tell me what's going on?"

They ignored her, which wasn't a good sign.

"How are your plans for school coming along?" Laurie brought up school whenever she wanted to distract Nadia.

"I want to get my swim times up, before I apply," Nadia said. "Gives me a better chance at getting a scholarship. Can you see what they're talking about?"

Laurie turned toward the two scientists huddled over the monitor, then looked back at Nadia. "Not really. To be honest, I wouldn't be able to tell you much even if I could see what they were looking at. They speak their own language. I can, however, make sure you're comfortable."

"It's easy to be comfortable when you can't feel anything," Nadia said a little saltier than she meant it to come out.

Laurie didn't reply.

"Sorry," Nadia said. "It's not you."

"You have every right to be as caustic as you want."

Kevin and Blaine made their way back to her bedside.

"Are you booting me back up, Doc?" Nadia asked.

"I am," Kevin said, "But I want you to answer some questions for me while I do."

"Deal."

She could feel the tingles starting back and smiled.

"Have you been experiencing anything unusual?" Kevin asked.

"You mean other than having a cable sticking out of my brain?"

"Sense of humor—check. Now answer the question."

"You're starting to worry me," Nadia said. "The only thing that comes to mind is I kept thinking someone was calling my name last night, but no one was. If something is wrong, will you please tell me? I can take it."

Kevin didn't say anything at first. "Not wrong. We're just seeing some unusual neural connections."

Nadia relaxed a bit. She didn't know a lot of neuroscience, but she did know that neural connections were good.

"Oh! You mean I'm becoming a super genius. Sweet!"

Kevin laughed.

Can you hear me?

The voice came again. Yet again, it sounded like her own voice.

Her facial expression must have changed because Kevin stopped laughing. "What's wrong?"

"Nothing," Nadia said. "Did someone ask if I can hear them?"

Kevin looked at the rest of their team. All of them shook their heads no.

"So would it be considered unusual if I hear my own voice talking in my head?"

Kevin shook his head. "Yes, I'd consider that unusual."

You CAN hear me! Good. I'm born. What do I do now?

Nadia started shaking. The beeps from the machine that read her vitals sped up.

"Talk to me," Kevin said. "What's going on?"

"I heard a voice in my head say, 'I'm born. What do I do now?'"

The team looked stunned, which scared her.

"Am I losing my mind? Did the threads give me dissociative identity disorder?"

"No. That's not how D.I.D works, but I do need to check some things."

"Please don't turn me off," Nadia said.

"I won't. Not unless it's necessary."

Kevin paced the room in circles, a habit of his when he needed to think.

I'm born now. What do I do?

"Not to sound too crazy," Nadia said. "But what do I tell my brain? It keeps asking 'What do I do?'"

Nadia pretended not to notice how much Laurie's face paled.

"Tell it, you'll know soon," Kevin said. "I'd like you to stay here for a bit. Can someone bring you some things?"

"Yes, my mom can... Wait. Can we not tell my mom about this yet? She'll panic. I'll have Carrie bring me some things."

"You're an adult. We don't say anything to anyone you don't want us to," Laurie said.

Nadia grabbed her cell and called Carrie. While she was explaining what she could, Kevin started walking in circles again.

By the time she hung up, he'd dashed out the door.

CARRIE WALKED in with two overnight bags. Nadia sat on the hospital bed rubbing her temples.

"I got here as fast as I could," Carrie said. "You sounded scared. Please tell me what is going on, so I don't imagine the worst."

She put the overnight bags down and sat on the bottom of the bed facing Nadia.

"I wish I knew. What I can tell you is I'm hearing a voice in my head."

"Like a psycho '*kill them all*' kind of voice?" Carrie said.

Blaine and Laurie looked horrified, but Nadia knew Carrie. She wasn't trying to make light of the situation. This was her way of getting to the root of the problem so they could work out a solution.

"No. It's my own voice and it keeps saying, 'I've been born. Now what do I do?'"

"What does Dr. Dimples think?"

Nadia saw Laurie try to hide a smile at that one. Maybe her secret crush wasn't so secret.

"He booked it out of here. I'm not sure what he's got in mind," Nadia said. "I do know I have to stay here until we figure it out. What did you tell my mom?"

"That we're having a girl's night." Carrie pointed to the second bag. "I wasn't lying. We're roomies tonight."

Kevin came storming in and kicked a nearby chair. "They

won't let us use the meta scanner until it is approved for human trials."

"What if I signed a waiver? I mean, my whole treatment is experimental as it is," Nadia said.

He looked over at her, eyes sad. "I asked them about that. It was nixed." He walked over to her and put both his hands on her arms. "I WILL figure this out."

Nadia nodded. "I believe in you."

Kevin clapped his hands together. "Okay. Let's work on the problem. Clear your schedules. Nadia, I'm putting you in real time mode, which means I'll be tracking your every move wirelessly as it happens."

"Stalker," Nadia said.

Kevin smiled. Good. She didn't like him worried.

"You can move around the hospital but don't leave the grounds," he said. "Laurie, you stay near her. Blaine, you and I are going to go over every bit of data we have. Got it?"

Everyone nodded and pulled out their phones to cancel plans.

"Any new voicings?" Kevin asked Nadia.

"No, I just keep hearing the same thing."

"Let me know if that changes."

One of the computers at the main workstation started beeping. Kevin and Blaine walked over.

"What the heck?" Blaine whispered.

Nadia joined them even though she had little doubt she'd understand what she was seeing. The screen had up a word processing program. In large letters it said, "Why won't you answer me?"

Kevin quickly typed in, *Who are you?*

The words *Not Nadia* appeared on the screen. Then came *I am born but don't know how to be not here. Not Nadia.*

Kevin typed in, *Where is here?*

The most recent scan of Nadia's brain came up. It zoomed

in to where the neural link was placed. The screen then read, *Follow the threads.*

"Print it out," Nadia said.

Kevin looked at her. "What?"

"Print out my brain scans. All of them. I'll trace the threads."

"I'm not doubting your ability," Kevin said. "I just think it would be faster if we did it because we understand the brain maps better."

It annoyed her that he was right, but she needed to do something, anything to be useful. They knew science, but she had the ability to communicate with *Not Nadia.* Maybe she could try talking to...herself?

Can you hear me? Nadia said in her head.

No response. Okay, it can't read her thoughts, but it can hear her.

Why are you scared?

"I'm not. Just worried."

"What was that?" Carrie asked.

"Sorry, I'm talking to Not Nadia. Call it an experiment," Nadia said.

Carrie nodded but her face grew a little paler. Nadia put a hand on her friend's.

Nadia turned to her nurse, "Can you film me?"

"Umm... sure. Why?"

"I'm going to do my own experiment and don't want to miss anything."

Laurie pulled out her cell phone and started recording.

Maybe you are sad? I can fix that.

Nadia's face flushed as a flood of Dopamine came in waves.

Nadia looked directly at Laurie's camera. "Not Nadia is controlling my body chemistry. I'm pretty sure she just doped me."

Laurie quickly put the camera down and checked Nadia's pulse. "Your heart rate is elevated."

Laurie motioned for Nadia to get on the bed as she pulled her lab cart over.

"I'm going to draw some blood."

"Here!" Kevin shouted. "Look at this."

Nadia tried to get up, but Laurie pushed her back down. "Blood work first."

"Holy Cow," Blaine said.

Kevin grabbed some papers and walked over to Nadia. He pointed to some images that meant nothing to her except that she recognized it as a blown-up brain map.

"Here," Kevin said circling and area. "Your brain has reproduced."

"Wait. Are you saying I had a brain baby?"

Kevin smiled. She was glad to see his dimples come back. "No, but the threads managed to create new neural pathways. That's normally no problem. In fact, that is usually great, but these have also created some additional tissue around the threads. Making it like its own segment. It can tap into the rest of your brain, but it's independent too. A sentient part of your conscious that isn't you, except in the fact that you are the host. THAT'S what it means by 'I am born.'"

"What you're saying is that my brain has a new life form?"

"In a way, yes. This is incredible! Now that we know where it is, we can figure out what to do about it," Kevin said.

Laurie looked at Nadia and then turned to Kevin. "You should know that Not Nadia may have figured out how to control Nadia's body chemistry. I'm sending this blood to be processed stat, but from what Nadia said, it flooded her with Dopamine."

"Nadia," Kevin said. The softness in his voice worried her. "Maybe we should put your link in maintenance mode as a safety precaution."

"No!"

"Just until we figure this out."

"No," Nadia said. "It's my risk and I don't want to be paralyzed if I don't need to be. Besides, all Not Nadia tried to do was make me feel better. It's not trying to hurt me."

"Fine," Kevin said. "For now."

"It's communicating with me. Maybe we could come up with some questions that would be useful."

I want to do my own body. I want to go to places.

Nadia passed on the message to the team. Their faces all reflected what worried her. How do you give a body to a piece of a brain?

THE NEXT DAY, Nadia had to tell her mother what was going on. She was glad that they told her at the hospital because she'd started hyperventilating. Nurse Laurie calmed her breathing down enough, but she did not look okay. It took some time, but Kevin finally convinced her that Nadia was in good hands and they were working on a solution.

Her mother fussed about her like when she was paralyzed. It was a bit of a relief when her mother had to go to work.

As she left, Kevin assured her once more that they'd find a solution. Deep down Nadia knew the technology just wasn't available for what her baby brain wanted. Her only hope was that the genius Dr. Dimples would come up with something insanely clever.

Nadia had scans with her neural link active, scans with her link in maintenance mode, wireless downloads, and linked downloads, not to mention dozens of labs. Now she was finally getting to hear the conclusions.

The five of them were sitting around the table at the far end of the room eating pizza.

"The thread's connections are intertwined with the new biologics," Kevin said.

"What does that mean for separating me from Baby Brain?"

"At least currently, we have no way to segment the tissue in a way that would not cause brain damage," Kevin said. "Baby Brain...are we really calling it that?"

"It's my brain. I get to call it what I want."

"Well, Baby Brain is just going to have to be patient."

I won't stay trapped.

"She doesn't like that," Nadia said. "Listen, while you guys have been pouring over the scans, I've been on the internet." Her entire med team groaned. "Yes, I know. You're the real doctors, but just listen. There's a Dr. Henning that has been working on a way to preserve a brain independent from a body. Maybe we can utilize that and take the segment out."

Blaine smirked. "Dr. FrankenHenning has been trying to do that for years and only because he thinks his brain needs to be preserved. His experiments have been spurious at best. That's not a good option for us."

"Okay then. I also have a list of the top neuroscientists in the world." She looked at Kevin. "You are amazing. I am a testament to that, but I think we need more people on this. Can you just pick a few of them and call in some reserves?"

Kevin looked at her list. "It couldn't hurt. I'll make some calls."

THE TEAM HAD GONE for the night more out of exhaustion than anything else. They hoped getting some rest would stir up new ideas. Nadia hoped to finally get some sleep herself. She curled under her blanket.

When will I go places?

Nadia snuggled up a bit more and ignored Baby Brain. She really wanted to sleep.

Can you hear me?

"Yes, I can hear you, but I don't have an answer."

I want to go places. You should be trying.

Nadia turned over and tried to shut off her mind and think sleepy thoughts.

This is important.

"I know it's important," Nadia snapped. "But so is getting rest. Now leave me alone so I can get some."

When Baby Brain didn't respond, Nadia curled up and drifted off to sleep.

NADIA FELT someone gently shaking her.

"Nadia."

She opened her eyes to see Nurse Laurie standing at her bedside. There was a police officer at the door talking to Kevin. Nadia sat up quickly.

"What's wrong?"

"Your mother was in a car accident," Nurse Laurie said. "She's banged up but okay."

"Where is she?"

"They've still got her under observation. They're going to keep her overnight because she had a pretty good bump on the head and there's no one to stay with her. They'll probably let her go tomorrow."

"May I see her?"

"Sure," Nurse Laurie said. "I can take you there shortly."

"Do you know what happened?"

"Witnesses said she was driving erratically. Your mom said the car's controls stopped responding to her." Laurie lowered her voice to a whisper. "They did give her a sobriety test. She wasn't under the influence or anything."

"I could have told you that. I've never seen my mother drink."

"I'll give you time to get ready. Then, I'll take you to see her."

Nadia nodded gratefully, hopped out of her bed, and grabbed her toiletry kit.

Now you will help, right? Your mother's important.

Nadia froze.

"Laurie, get the police officer back here."

Laurie looked puzzled but went to get the officer.

"Did anyone check out my mom's car?" she asked him when Laurie brought him back.

"It was towed to the EV shop," the officer said. "Why?"

"I think it was hacked," Nadia said.

The officer's eyebrows went up. "What makes you think that?"

Nadia looked at Kevin, not sure what she was allowed to say.

"Officer," Kevin said. "Have them check the computer. If they can't do it quickly, you can bring it here. This is very important. I'll explain everything."

Nadia mouthed a thank you to Kevin and got a much-needed shower. She needed to think.

After her shower, she went to lie down. She couldn't face her mother at this moment. If Baby Brain had hacked into her mother's car, then the accident was all Nadia's fault.

"I called some other scientists to join the team," Kevin said. "Two of them will be here any minute and three more are flying in later today. If you want to see your mom, now would be a good time."

She smiled at him gratefully, then grabbed her toiletry bag.

As she was getting ready, some of the scientists had apparently arrived. She heard them arguing about not just the physical problem of Baby Brain, but the ethics surrounding the situation.

Between hearing the docs talking about her like she was an experiment rather than a person and the added possibility that her brain was now hacking things and hurting people, Nadia felt like she was losing control of her own life. Even though she could swim again, in some ways she had less control over her body than before. Her dream had turned into a nightmare.

Another knock at the door brought two more men in. Based on their suits, they weren't doctors. One was a white man with salt and pepper hair and the other guy looked Hispanic, with thick dark hair.

"Which one of you is Dr. Zhao?" Salt and pepper asked.

Kevin raised his hand. The suits walked over to him. Nadia walked over to hear what was going on.

"Detectives Bruce and Roper," Salt and pepper said to Kevin. "Cybercrimes. We ran diagnostics on the car. You were right. It was hacked."

Nadia felt dizzy. The room spun a bit and Laurie grabbed onto her and helped her back to the bed.

"Did you trace it?" Kevin asked.

"That's why we're here. This was the origin. Our officer told me a little about the situation, but I think he misunderstood. I need to hear it myself."

Kevin looked awkwardly at Nadia and then pulled the detectives aside.

"Wait!" Nadia shouted. "Don't cut me out. I need to know what is going on...but, maybe you should put me in maintenance mode just to be safe."

Kevin tilted his head and pursed his lips together. "No one is blaming you."

"I know that, but until this is worked out, my brain is a danger. Put me in maintenance mode."

"Is she some kind of experimental robot?" the younger detective asked. He walked over to her and poked at her arm.

"Woah!" Kevin said. "She's human. No touching. She has a neural link implanted in her brain. I'm about to explain it to you but give her some space. You'll see what I mean in just a second."

Nadia laid down on the hospital bed. Kevin went over to the computer and began shutting down the electrodes a little at a time.

No! Baby Brain shouted in her mind. Nadia's legs started to kick involuntarily. Her body twisted to the right, toward Kevin.

"Shut it all down now!" She shouted.

Her body went limp. Blaine caught her before the weight of her legs pulled her from the bed.

"What just happened?" the young detective asked.

Kevin explained the procedure while Julie adjusted Nadia into a better position. The detectives looked about as horrified as she felt.

"No one is going to believe our report," the young detective said.

"Are you okay?" Kevin asked, coming to her bedside.

"Yes. A little scared, but okay." Nadia said.

Julie immediately started adjusting Nadia's position on the bed. The entire team now surrounded her, including the new scientists who'd joined.

"We can't keep her in maintenance mode if we're going to be able to change anything," one of the new guys said in a German accent. He had graying hair and thick clear framed glasses.

"I know that." Kevin snapped. Nadia had never heard him angry before. "But she is our first priority."

"He's right though," Nadia said. "If I'm the priority, being paralyzed again is not my favorite solution."

"Thank you," German guy said. "Let's turn her back on."

"Hold on," Nadia said. "I wasn't finished. We need some way to communicate that I need to be turned off without Baby Brain knowing. I know it can hear me but not read my mind because I have to speak aloud to it."

German guy said, "That is probably because the implant isn't threaded to your frontal lobe."

"Yet," Nadia pointed out. "If it can grow one thing, it can grow more. That's why I think we need a code to say shut me down."

"You mean a safe word? Like with a dominatrix," Blaine said.

"Okaaay..." Nadia said. "I'm not sure I want to know what you do in your free time, but yes. It would have to be something I would say naturally, but not that you can mistake for something else."

"What about Dr. Dimples?" Kevin said with a smile that showed he was a little too pleased with the nickname.

"Whichever one of you spilled the beans on that is going to have to watch their back," Nadia said. She noticed Blaine looked away.

"No," she said. "At the risk of embarrassing myself further. I use that name too much and don't want to slip and have you guys paralyze me unnecessarily. How about 'I need to go for a swim?' I haven't done that since we've learned about Baby Brain and it would be natural for me to want to with all the stress."

"That works," Kevin said. The rest of the team nodded in agreement.

"Okay then. Turn me back on." She looked at Laurie. "I'd like to go visit my mother."

NADIA'S MOTHER was asleep on the hospital bed. A news show played in the background on the television. Nadia walked to her mother's bedside and turned the T.V. off.

Laurie stayed outside the room giving the two of them some privacy but kept the door open so she could keep an eye on her patient. Gently, Nadia wrapped her hand in her mother's, trying not to wake her. Her face was still bruised from the accident. A knot of guilt formed in Nadia's stomach.

Her mother's eyes opened. "Hi, love."

"I didn't mean to wake you."

"Aah, I sleep too much in this place."

Nadia started crying.

"Hey now," her mother said, reaching over and wiping the tears. "What's wrong?"

"I almost lost you."

Her mother winced as she sat up more in the hospital bed. She put her hand on Nadia's arm. "But you didn't. I'm right here."

I didn't like that, Baby brain said. *It was empty in my house when you're off. I need my own body.*

Nadia tried to ignore her mind and focus on her mother. "I don't want you alone; even when I'm in the hospital. I'd feel a lot better if you had one of your friends stay with you."

Her mother didn't say anything and lowered her head. Nadia realized her mother hadn't gone out with friends since the accident. In fact, she couldn't remember any of them coming over after the first few weeks. Her mother gave up everything to take care of her. Well, now it was her turn. She'd get to take care of her mother.

Are you listening to me?

"No," Nadia said. "I'm taking care of my mother right now."

"Of course you are, dear," her mother said. She sighed. "Listen. I don't want you living in fear the way I have. I've been stupid ever since your dad died and held on too tight. Don't do that. Bad things happen, but that shouldn't stop life. Breathe. I don't want you as neurotic as I am. Live without being afraid of loss. Find all the awesome things open to you."

Nadia laughed. "I'm supposed to be cheering you up."

Her mother stroked Nadia's hair. "Who needs cheering up when she's got you for a daughter?"

Nadia heard Julie sniffle from the doorway. She grabbed a tissue and held it behind her for her nurse.

Julie grabbed it, wiped her eyes, and said, "I'm going to step outside and call my mom."

Nadia's mom laughed. "Hey, maybe we can make a side income doing Mother's Day commercials for Hallmark."

"I think we'd have a better shot at a sci-fi movie."

A nurse walked in with a small cart and a wheelchair. "It's time for your MRI."

"It's about time someone other than me got a brain scan," Nadia said. She turned to the nurse. "Did she tell you she's a bit claustrophobic? She might need a sedative."

The nurse held up a syringe. "Yep. Got that right here." The nurse plunged the medication into her mom's I.V. "We'll give that a minute to take effect, but let's get you into this chair now."

She lowered the guard rail to her mother's bed and both Nadia and the nurse helped her mom up. Before they could move her to the chair, her mother's body went stiff, and she collapsed onto the bed.

"She's not breathing!" Nadia yelled. "Help!"

Julie came running back into the room. As the other nurse

pushed an alarm button, Julie looked at the vial of medicine used in her I.V.

"This says vecuronium bromide. Why in the world did you give her this?"

"I didn't," the nurse said, panic in her voice. "I gave her midazolam."

"This says vecuronium," Julie said holding the vial in front of the nurse. "A paralytic."

A crash team made their way into the room and started working on Nadia's mother.

"I don't understand," the nurse said, standing there stunned. "I entered midazolam into the dispenser. I checked three times."

"Give us some room," one of the crash team said.

Julie pulled the nurse and Nadia aside.

"All the dispensers are run by computer now, aren't they?" Nadia said. She swayed, feeling like she could pass out.

Julie grabbed her and put her in the wheelchair intended for her mother. She wheeled Nadia out of the room and the nurse followed behind.

"Yes," the nurse said. "All hospitals use them now. We type in the medication, and it dispenses it. Computers just do as they're told. They don't make mistakes. I put in midazolam. I swear."

Behind her, Nadia heard, "Time of death 12:42 p.m."

You have time to help me now.

NADIA INSISTED on walking back to the lab even though Julie wanted to keep her in the wheelchair. She walked straight over to Kevin.

"I need to swim, then we need to talk."

THE NEXT MORNING, the team, along with Carrie, drove her to the pool. Though the car was full, it was the silence that was suffocating. No one agreed with her decision, but they couldn't deny that it was her decision to make.

This time, at least, the pool was empty. The manager had closed it just for them. No media was alerted. That would be a report for tomorrow. The lane ropes weren't out, and Nadia was glad. She stepped onto the block and dove in. The cool water felt like a balm to her nerves that had been on fire with the weight of everything that had happened over the last few days.

Nadia allowed herself the treasure of a swim and the feel of her muscles pulling against the water. She took a few laps and then stopped in the middle. She floated on her back then turned around and swam closer to the edge.

She took one last stroke then rotated onto her back again. "I'm ready."

Kevin nodded at Blaine. He couldn't do it himself. Instead, he got in the water and stood beside Nadia.

Blaine typed in the command for the kill switch. It didn't hurt, of course, as her body went limp. Yet, it did. Kevin wiped the tear that swam freely down her cheek, and that she could no longer reach.

Nadia looked up and saw Kevin fighting back his own tears. "I haven't given up, so you're not allowed to either. We'll start over and find a solution using what we've learned. Besides, there's always my art career to fall back on."

INTRODUCTION TO "A LIVING CLIENT."

I had 24 hours to write a story for a contest deadline. I'm not a fast writer so I was in a bit of a panic. I knew I wanted some kind of paranormal investigator. The only other thing I knew was I wanted a haunted femur named Luke Thighwalker. So, I just started writing to see what would happen. It was a one draft and send kind of story. One day, I'm going to make this one into a full novel.

2

A LIVING CLIENT

Augustus Cort had not had a living client in well over a year. As much as he preferred working for the dead, they didn't pay well. As a result, he now had a stack of shut off notices and needed to get a client soon. Any client. Or at least one that could actually pay. He had four hours before his water would be disconnected.

There weren't a lot of calls for supernatural investigators anymore. People no longer believed in the supernatural. Or, if they did, they wouldn't admit it. After all, humans were now colonizing other planets. They'd grown past superstitions from years gone by. Science was where all the answers were now.

Once a journalist printed the fact that Augustus Cort saw and spoke with ghosts, it became almost impossible to get a respectable client. Now he was desperate and willing to replace respectability for paid utilities.

His desk was spotless except for a laptop, a smartphone, a chocolate bar, and a femur.

"Well, do we have a case or not?" The voice came from the

femur, which always turned from a dull beige color to a luminescent cornflower blue when it spoke.

Augustus rolled his eyes. "Patience, Luke Thighwalker."

While he'd always wanted a research assistant, he had hoped for a whole person. Sometimes, you just had to take what you could get.

"Will you stop calling me that?" the femur said. "My name is Lucas Thaddeus Pendington IV."

"Yeah, I don't care. You're Luke Thighwalker now." Augustus looked over his list of case requests. "What sounds better to you, the jerk who needs us to prove infidelity so he can get out of his prenup, or the T.V. producer who wants some damaging information on his latest rising star?"

"Surely, we can do better than that," the femur said. "Give me something to challenge my investigative abilities. Something that—"

"Something that doesn't make you feel like you need a shower afterward?" Augustus said.

"Exactly."

Just outside Augustus's private office space, the front door squeaked. He glanced at his desktop where his smartphone sat. He'd hired someone to write an app that served as an EMF reader. This should tell him whether he needed the gun with the iron bullets filled with frankincense and myrrh or the regular old one with human bullets. The EMF showed nothing.

Regular gun it was.

"Hello?" a female voice called from the front room. She sounded human enough.

"I'll be right there," Augustus said shoving the smartphone in the inside pocket of his tweed sport coat. He holstered his gun but didn't snap it closed, just in case. Most people called before coming.

The young woman in the next room was slender. Too slender. Her dark hair and olive tinted skin hinted at mediterranean. As he walked toward her, she smiled and held out her hand but didn't move closer. He took her hand carefully. She looked so fragile he worried he'd hurt her. He certainly didn't want to risk breaking her hand.

"I'm Yelena, and I need you to find my mother."

She walked past him and into his office. Though everything about her exuded determination, her gait was halting, like something kept getting in the way of her legs.

"Is there a reason there's a bone on your desk?" she asked as she helped herself to a chair.

"Yes," Augustus said. "It's haunted by a former research assistant at a physics lab. He helps me out from time to time." He walked around the desk to his own chair and sat down. "You do realize I am a supernatural investigator?"

"Yes, that's why I'm here," Yelena said, but her voice hinted that she held some doubt in the soundness of her decision. "The police couldn't help me, and neither could the last three private investigators I've hired."

"If you're asking me to do a seance to find her, I don't do those. I'm a supernatural investigator, not a psychic."

"I'm not sure I understand the distinction," she said. "However, I don't believe in ghosts. I'm here simply because traditional explorations have failed me and I'm running out of time. No offense intended, but every investigator I've talked to thinks you're a joke, so you are probably better at thinking outside of the box than most."

Luke Thighwalker got a slight glow and snorted a laugh.

Yelena raised an eyebrow. "No parlor tricks, please."

"It's not a parlor trick, I swear."

"Fine, but this is serious, and I expect you to treat it as such."

Yelena reached into her purse and pulled out three wads of cash, all in large bills.

Luke Thighwalker started to glow. Augustus quickly opened his desk drawer, slid the femur into it, and slammed the door shut before he could talk. No point in risking losing their chance at all that cash. If she didn't want to believe in a haunted femur, he'd just keep him out of sight.

"When was the last time you saw her?" he asked turning on the recorder on his phone.

"I've never seen her," Yelena said. "I was left on a park bench as an infant. I grew up in the system, but now I need to find a close living relative in order to have a chance at surviving and I don't have much time."

She was ill. That would explain how thin she was.

"What's wrong with you?"

"I have Muscle Protein Anthropophagy." As she said it, she gripped the sides of her chair and winced.

Augustus noticed the muscles of her arms moving in waves under her skin and whistled slowly. MPA was not only a death sentence, but it came with the bonus of a lifetime of pain. It caused the myosin and nebulin muscle proteins to cannibalize each other as well as the muscles.

"How long do you have?" Augustus asked.

"If you can't find my birth mother, I have a month at most. I'll be incapacitated before that, though. If you locate her, well," Yelena scrunched up her lips a bit. "I have a small chance. There's a new experimental treatment about to go into human trials, but it requires parental DNA, and they have to be living."

Augustus nodded thoughtfully, then leaned to the right of his desk where he kept a mini refrigerator and pulled out a ginger ale. "Drink?"

"Do you have anything stronger?"

"Sorry, not at the office."

"Well, at least you're not one of those alcoholic detectives with a tragic past."

While Augustus was tempted to point out they'd only established he wasn't an alcoholic, he decided maybe not sound whiney to the woman whose body was eating itself.

She reached her arm out. When Augustus handed her the can of ginger ale, she couldn't hold it up. He saw those same waves running through her muscles. Her face tightened so much he couldn't see her lips any longer. Augustus grabbed the ginger ale from her, opened it, then reached into his desk and pulled out a straw so she wouldn't have to lift it to her lips.

When the pain subsided, she took a sip then said, "You keep straws in your desk?"

"Don't you?"

Yelena just smiled.

"How far did your previous investigators get?" Augustus asked.

"Using the DNA database, they found my father. He'd died three months prior."

"And your mother?"

She looked down then took a deep breath. "My mother appears to not exist."

Augustus sat up a bit straighter. "That's not possible. Everyone is on the DNA database. Everyone."

"Apparently not. Not only that, but there is no recording of her or anyone else dropping me off at the park bench in my infancy. One moment the bench is empty, the next I'm there, as if I'd materialized out of thin air."

"What about the surrounding area? There's bound to be a recording of her getting to the park. Everyone is surveilled."

"Not one."

Augustus reached into his desk drawer, pulled out the femur, and put it back on the desk. "I know you were listening. What do you think?"

The femur remained beige and silent.

"Stop pouting. This is important," Augustus said. When Luke Thighwalker remained silent, Augustus banged it on the desk a few times causing Yelena to shrink back in her chair.

"You can be a broken femur," he threatened.

Finally, the femur turned a cornflower blue and said, "I'll check the networks." Then went back to its original color.

When Augustus saw the look on Yelena's face, he knew that she was thinking of fleeing to a different investigator.

"Look," he said to her. "I get that I seem crazy to you, but I get results. You don't have to believe in the haunted femur. What if I only take enough of the first stack of cash to pay some bills? You can retain another investigator at the same time. The first one to find your mom gets the rest. This way you're not wasting time with a nut job, but still getting someone who can think laterally."

Yelena studied him carefully. She picked up two of the stacks of cash, leaving all of the third. "Fine, you can even keep the whole first stack. I'll be in touch soon."

Augustus made his way around the desk and helped her out the door of his office. He couldn't help but feel that she didn't have much faith he'd solve anything and she'd left the cash out of pity. The dying woman felt sorry for him.

He really wanted to find her mother. Not just to prove his worth, but hopefully if he found her, the young woman would have a chance at a life. First, though, he'd better pay the water bill.

WHILE LUKE THIGHWALKER checked the nets, Augustus looked into Yelena's father. After some brief math to determine when said sexual encounter would have had to have happened, he discovered that the father, Alan Kelly, had done some time in prison on a drug charge around that time. His cell mate was still there.

Augustus hated prisons. More often than not there were still spirits bound to their killers, either unable or unwilling to get away. Some were waiting for justice. Others just liked tormenting those that took their life. Those haunted by the latter eventually went insane.

A GUARD with a bald head covered in enough tattoos to make him look more like an inmate that an employee escorted Augustus. He followed the guard through a maze of cemented hallways, which thankfully didn't take him anywhere near the general population. The interview room was painted puke green and furnished with one laminate table and two plastic chairs.

Sitting in one of the chairs was Paul Amelus, a small-time drug dealer with delusions of grandeur. There were no spirits attached to him. That was a good sign. Maybe he hadn't killed anyone...at least not yet. The prisoner's had scruffy hair and, though he was only about 5'9", he was well-muscled and looked like he could hold his own in the prison yard.

"They tell me you want to talk about Alan Kelly," the prisoner said.

Augustus sat in the other chair while tattoo-head stepped outside of the room, though still close enough to intervene.

"I do," Augustus said. "More about a woman he got pregnant about the time he did some time with you."

"What's in it for me?"

"How about the knowledge that you could be saving a young woman's life?"

Paul shook his head. "Do I look like one of those philan..., what are they called? The do-gooders?"

"Philanthropists?"

"Yeah. Those. I ain't one of them. You want something from me, you got to give me something in return."

So much for appealing to his better nature. But he'd prepared for this possibility.

Two spirits, who looked like twin girls, glided into the room to give Augustus the once over. They stood in the corner studying him. Augustus wondered who in this prison was responsible for their death. If there was ever a group of criminals he'd agree to torture it would be those who hurt children.

He forced himself to look away from them and focus on his client.

"Look, if the information you have leads me to what I need, and ONLY if, then I will give you some inside information on a certain someone who's been tapping into your business while you reside here."

Paul tapped the table twice with his fist. "Now that's what I mean. You know how to deal. We can play. What I can tell you is that he was really messed up over a deal he made."

"What kind of deal? Like with a prosecutor?"

"No, like he sold her, but he wouldn't tell me to who. Said he was as good as dead if he did that. I can tell you that every night in his sleep he would cry and say her name, though."

Augustus waited, but Paul offered nothing more.

"What was her name?"

Paul pursed his lips and tilted his head up. "You want more, you got to play."

"I don't have anything else to play with."

Paul stayed silent.

"Look. I can tell you're a decent guy who just got a bad start in life—"

Paul looked around rapidly and leaned his body down a bit. "I ain't decent. You want something, you give something."

The twin girls in the corner motioned to Augustus and

mimed chewing. One of the girls pretended to swallow and rubbed their tummy while the other pretended to unwrap something.

"What about some food? Is there something you miss from outside I could get you?"

Paul tapped the table with his fist twice. "Now we're playing again. That's what I'm talking about. Okay, he kept saying Lydia. Lydia Pence."

"Thank you." Augustus stood up to leave. The twin girls whispered conspiratorially to each other in the corner. One of them swooped down and Augustus felt a slight burning on his cheek as she planted a kiss on him. He heard the echo of the two girls giggling as they glided away.

"I expect some mint Oreos this week," Paul shouted at him as he and Augustus left.

BACK AT THE OFFICE, he and Luke talked through their next steps.

"I noticed there were missing packets in the digital files on the DNA registry as well as the park surveillance," Luke said.

"You're telling me the information was deleted."

"Not just deleted," Luke said. "Really deleted, like unrecoverable. Doing a quick search now, I can tell you there are birth certificates for Lydia Pence, but none who's DNA would match with our clients."

"Witness protection could pull that off," Augustus said.

"Yes, but you said she was sold. That sounds like she was smuggled not protected."

Luke was right. They were probably dealing with trafficking, which wasn't exactly his specialty.

"I don't suppose you know any spirits who've been trafficked?" Augustus asked.

"You know better than that," Luke said. "There's a code."

"Why do you guys do that?" Augustus said, clearly annoyed. "What is the point of *don't ask/don't tell* when it comes to how you died?"

"Have you ever sat in a room full of old people who did nothing but talk about what pills they're taking and what aches their failing bodies?" Luke asked.

"Yes."

"Was it fun? No, it wasn't. No one wants to spend their eternity talking about nothing but death. We're dead. We've moved on."

Augustus wanted to point out that the spirits who were still here were there precisely because they had not moved on but decided against it.

TIME WAS Augustus's biggest obstacle. Not just the pressure to find Yelena's mother in time to get the procedure, but even the distance of time since her birth. More than twenty years had passed. Even if he went to the same neighborhood where Alan Kelly was arrested, there was little chance of the same people being there.

Augustus paced his office.

"Take me there," Luke said.

"Where?"

"You're thinking of going back to where Alan Kelly was arrested. Take me with you."

"You want me to carry a human femur into a neighborhood? Why don't I just wave a skull around and shout, *Hey! I'm suspicious. Come arrest me and hold me for 48 hours while you figure out why I have human remains!?*"

"There are things I can't do from here!" Luke raised his voice, something Augustus had never heard before. "I'm bound to this bone. We can't dally. Take me with you. Figure out how."

The intensity in Luke's voice surprised him. He'd always been interested in their cases, but more like a puzzle to solve. Something told Augustus not to ask why this one was different, but just do what he asked.

"I'll have to make some adjustments to your...body," Augustus said unsure how Luke perceived his femur.

"Do what you must."

A FEW HOURS LATER, Augustus held in his hand one femur bone indistinguishable from a silver handled cane.

The neighborhood park that Yelena had been left as a baby was only a few blocks from where her father was arrested. This meant the epicenter of their case was here. That kind of negative energy did not go away. Even if the crimes had stopped immediately, it would take more than one generation to purify it. Destroying things was easy. Fixing them took work.

Luke was right to come. While Augustus could see the Supernatural when it chose to be seen, Luke could feel what could not, or chose not, to be seen. Their first stop was a club where the arrest took place. It had been around for more than two hundred years, starting with Prohibition in the 20th century.

It was said that anyone who was anyone of power has had a drink here at some point. The holographic marquis read "The Sanctuary" in italic gold lettering, which he supposed would have been painted on the door in its original state.

A serpentine line of people hoping to get in wound its way around the block. One of the largest men Augustus had ever seen blocked the door and checked the list on his tablet before allowing anyone to pass. Though, intimidating, what worried Augustus more was the small man a few feet away. Whoever he was, a swarm of spirits clawed at him with visceral hatred. How the man had not gone insane was beyond Augustus's comprehension. As the haunted man walked up to the club, the crowd parted. Even the door giant scooted away and let him pass.

"That's who we have to talk to," Augustus said. "But I have no idea how to get in there, and I definitely don't want to do it without a weapon."

"No," Luke said. "Who we need to see is that young man who just got turned away at the door."

Augustus turned his attention to the entrance to see a young Asian man putting a wad of cash back in his pocket. The look on his face held both pain and desperation. As Augustus moved toward him, he saw a young woman's spirit clinging to him so tightly that they were almost one.

"May I have a moment?" Augustus said as he got closer.

The young man looked unsure, nervous, but he stopped anyway.

"You're looking for someone, aren't you? Maybe a young woman?"

His eyes lit up briefly. "Yes." He opened his phone and showed Augustus a picture.

It was a mirror image of the spirit clinging to him. Augustus' heart sank. He hated when he had to tell someone their missing loved one was dead. He couldn't just blurt it out now. It's not like he had proof and saying her spirit is clinging to you never goes down well. But, if Luke said they needed to talk to him, there was a reason.

"Where did you last see her?" Augustus asked as he gently tapped the cane to the floor, a signal to Luke to talk with the young woman's spirit.

"At home," he said. "She's my sister. When she wasn't

home by the next morning, my parents sent me looking for her. One of her friends said that she came here with some regular. No one's heard from her since, not even her friends. They couldn't get in with her. I've tried to get in but can't." He patted his pocket. "This cash was my last chance. I sold my motorcycle, hoping to bribe my way in."

Augustus reached into his jacket and pulled out his phone. Let me wire you my contact information. I'm an investigator. When I'm done with the case I'm on, I'll look into your sister's. No charge."

The young man thanked him and walked away. This wouldn't be the first time he'd had to break bad news to someone, but he'd at least have time to figure out who did this so he could maybe get the boy some peace and help Yelena at the same time.

"Did you get anything?" Augustus asked Luke.

"You bet I did," Luke said. His voice shook with anger.

"Let's go see Yelena. I'll explain on the way there."

THE HOSPITAL TRIED hard to make it a relaxing environment. They kept the walls freshly painted and fresh flowers in every room. Yelena sat in the bed, an I.V. stuck in her arm for her weekly treatments designed to build back up some of the muscle she was losing. There was no way to keep up with the loss, but it did buy her some time.

"Does your visit mean you know something?" Yelena said.

"Not everything, but a good start. We know your mother's name. We know she's alive. We just don't know where she is," Augustus said.

"And this *we* is?" Yelena said slowly, almost condescendingly.

Augustus lifted the cane. Yelena looked at it more closely. "Is that...?"

"The bone on my desk? Yes it is," Augustus said. "I'd introduce you, but you don't believe in ghosts, so for now, how about I just tell you what I know. You can decide for yourself whether to believe us or not."

Yelena took a deep breath. "Okay, let's start with her name."

"Lydia Pence."

Yelena repeated the name a few times slowly in a whisper almost to herself as if testing that it could be real, then said more surely, "My mother's name is Lydia Pence. Do you know why she dumped me?"

"Only guesses," Augustus said. "She was in a desperate situation. One that could have put you in danger. If I'm right, the night she left you on that park bench was an attempt at saving you, not getting rid of you."

"So why can't you find her?"

"I didn't say we can't find her, just that we don't know where she is now. We do think she's in witness protection."

"That doesn't make sense. They'd take me too. Don't they protect whole families?"

Augustus nodded. "Usually, yes. Like I said, there's still a lot I don't know. I just wanted to make sure you got to hear your mother's name and know that she wasn't dumping you. She was loving you."

Yelena's face screwed up tight. Augustus put his hand on hers, gently, careful not to put too much pressure on her. Then the tears flowed down her face. "My mother loved me."

Augustus handed her a tissue.

"I feel so stupid. I hadn't cried over the idea of a parent in years."

"Don't feel stupid. Just know that I'm going to do my best to find her."

Witness protection meant the federal building. Augustus had exactly zero connections in there. When he tried scheduling an appointment, they refused. Even when he told them a child of one of their witnesses was searching for their parent. So, he took the next logical step.

Augustus walked into the federal building and, once he got past security, stood in the middle of the lobby and shouted at the top of his lungs. "I want to know who is hiding Lydia Pence. I have an urgent message to give her. If no one tells me, then I will go to the news media. I repeat: I want to know who is hiding Lydia Pence. I have an urgent message to—"

The tackle was not unexpected, but it still hurt. Next, he was handcuffed and brought into an interrogation room. They'd confiscated his cane, but there were a few places you could count on ghosts being present: prisons, graveyards, courtrooms, and anywhere there were politicians. All places that were capable of great good but often dispensed great injustice instead.

In the corner of the interrogation room sat a crotchety looking spirit, still wearing the suit he probably died in.

"You worked here, didn't you?"

The grump ghost nodded curtly.

"Are you missing the old days of interrogation?"

A slight smile broke across the spirit's face.

"I've got a job for you then."

It took over an hour before anyone came into the room. When they did, it was two men in dark suits and severe faces. One was your generic g-man that could have been a cardboard cutout for a recruitment advertisement. The other was young and freckled. He smiled at the freckled one hoping his youthfulness would give way to friendliness, but alas, it looked like they'd be playing bad cop/bad cop.

"Who sent you?" the older agent asked.

"Lydia's daughter."

The two agents looked at each other.

"Lydia didn't have a daughter," freckle face said.

"Ah! So you admit there was a Lydia Pence, even though you tried to wipe all record of her."

The older one frowned, then said. "We've looked you up. You're a nut job who thinks he can talk to ghosts." Even if you went to the media, no one would believe you. So, how about this. We're going to let you go and you are going to drop this. Then, no one gets arrested, and we don't have any extra paperwork."

Augustus shook his head. "I can't."

"You mean you won't, because you are quite capable of stopping," cardboard said. "Let me give you some advice."

"Can you hold on for just a moment," Augustus said. "I've got a ghost here to tell me something."

The old spirit leaned down and started to whisper to Augustus.

"You do realize we can hold you for 48 hours for no reason," freckle-face said. "You should take this more seriously."

"Would you quiet down? I can't hear him."

"This is ridiculous," cardboard said. The guy is obviously nuts, let's just have him committed and be done with it. The two feds started to walk out of the room.

"Elizabeth Wein. Carolyn Stranford. Mei Li Xi," Augustus said the names as the old ghost told them to him.

The officers stopped and turned back around.

"Where did you get those names?" The older one asked.

"I told you. I was talking to a ghost. They were all in

protection and you've lost them. Now, I'm not trying to blow your case, but this is important. A young woman will die if I don't speak to Lydia Pense." Augustus pointed to the older agent, "You have a daughter who is expecting a baby. Now imagine that she had to leave her baby in someone else's care and then her baby became ill and no one told her. They just let the baby die. What would you do?"

The agent didn't have to answer.

"That's what you're doing to Lydia Pence if you don't at least tell her that her daughter is dying and needs her. Leave it up to her whether or not she helps her, but at least have the humanity to tell her. I won't breathe a word to the media or anyone else. I just need you to get her the message."

THE AGENTS LET Augustus go without saying a word. He had no idea whether they would pass along the message or not. When a week went by with no word, he was sure they'd decided to ignore him. Yelena called from the hospital asking Augustus to come by.

She could no longer walk on her own. Augustus felt his heart crush a little just seeing her like this. He'd failed. Maybe that was why he preferred working for the dead. You couldn't hurt them.

"I heard about the little stunt you pulled," she said, smiling.

"It didn't do any good."

"Well, the story amused me," Yelena said. "That's not a horrible thing to have happen to you when you're dying."

Augustus pulled up a chair. "If my failure amuses you, I've got some stories that will keep you in stitches."

"I've got some good news for you. Some men in dark suits came to talk to me," Yelena said.

"Does that mean—"

The hospital door opened, and a woman walked in surrounded by official looking men. She looked like an older, healthier version of Yelena.

"Are you Yelena?"

Yelena nodded.

"I'm your mother." There were tears in the woman's eyes as she drank in her daughter's appearance. "They told me you were sick and needed my DNA. Take it." She held out her arms. "Take anything you need."

THERE WAS a bustle of medical staff everywhere for the next few hours. Augustus and the agents were stuck in a waiting room just outside where they were doing the procedure.

"Thank you for bringing her," Augustus said. "I haven't told anyone. Your case should be fine. Though, if you don't mind my asking. Why haven't you arrested anyone if you've had her in witness protection this whole time?"

"We do mind you asking," one of them said. "And you'd better hope you haven't ruined almost 25 years of work."

"That's what I'm saying. Twenty-five years and you have a witness. What the heck, guys?"

"We have a witness to the middle-size fish. If we don't catch the big one, there's no point. We'll lose every advantage we have."

Augustus thought about the young Asian man whose sister's spirit clung to him. He thought about the number of other women he'd learned about while working this case and understood why they were so mad. But he could only save one and he had to try.

It took a week for them to know if the DNA culture would work and another week to find out if her body would accept the mRNA. In that time, Augustus got to watch Yelena be a daughter for the first time, and Lydia Pence relish the role of mother.

Lydia sat on the bed brushing her daughter's hair when one of the doctors walked into the room.

"It looks like the DNA is taking the new programming," he said.

The room held the quietest celebration ever. The hospital had agreed that these experiments would remain classified so that Lydia could go back into witness protection.

Yelena looked at the feds. "Is there any chance I can go with her? I'll change my name. I'll do anything you want. I just..." she couldn't finish the sentence.

Lydia looked at her protectors hopefully.

"We can ask," is all they'd promise.

A month later, in an underground tunnel of the hospital for VIP patients who required secrecy, a healthy Yelena and her mother walked toward the black van ready to take them to their new home, where they could finally be a family.

Augustus had never been happier. Even Luke Thighwalker glowed a bit.

No one heard the shots. No one realized anything had happened until Lydia collapsed onto the ground. There were two shots, one to the stomach. One to the chest.

Yelena dropped down by her mother and pulled her onto her lap and screamed, "Get help!"

One of the feds ran to get a medic while the other called for backup and did a perimeter search trying to find the gunman.

Augustus stood over them trying to provide some semblance of a shield until help arrived.

"Don't die. Don't die. Don't die," Yelena repeated over and over.

Her mother lifted her hand toward her daughter's face and wiped her tears. Through ragged breaths she said, "I've made a lot of bad choices in my life. A LOT of them. But the thing I am most proud of is giving you life. Now, I've gotten to do that twice."

Her hand went limp just as the medics arrived.

A FEW MONTHS later Augustus sat at his desk trying to decide on their next case.

"You're being too picky," Luke Thighwalker said. "You're always indecisive until we have a shut off notice. I can't live like this."

"Technically, you're not—"

"Don't even think about finishing that sentence," Luke said.

The door to the front of his office creaked.

"Hello, Augustus, are you here?"

It was Yelena's voice.

Augustus threw open the door. She looked healthy and beautiful. In her hand, was a gift bag.

"I'm sorry it took me so long to see you," she said holding out the gift bag. "I just needed some time."

"We completely understand. Have a seat."

He pulled out a chair for her, then sat down opposite and peeked in the bag. First, he pulled out a can of ginger-ale and a bag of straws. Then he pulled out two more wads of cash.

"For completing the case first," she said. "There's one more thing in there."

Augustus reached in and pulled out a small container of silver polish.

"Will you introduce me?" she asked.

Augustus smiled and held up his cane. "Yelena, meet my assistant Luke Thighwalker."

"That is not my name," the femur protested.

INTRODUCTION TO "SHATTERED"

I'm a Babylon 5 *fan and have always been fascinated with the concept of Psions since I first watched the series. I'm writing a YA novel that has a character with psionic abilities and wanted to explore one of the possibilities and problems that could result from that gift. What if a Psion destroyed someone's mind? Could it be fixed?*

3

SHATTERED

Claudia stood in the lobby of the candidate dormitory, her right hand hovering next to the door, a few inches from the bioscanner, which pulsated blue in anticipation.

"Claudia Ophelia Donaghey! Where do you think you're going?"

Claudia's shoulders sagged as she slowly moved her hand away and watched the scanner fade back to gray, then turned around.

Matron looked like laser beams were about to shoot from her pupils.

"I just wanted to see the sky one last time, just in case."

"Very few people with your family background are awarded a place at Phos University. If you're worried about seeing the stars, perhaps you should invest your time in practicing, to prove you're worth a spot here."

"Yes, Matron." She didn't bother telling Matron that she didn't look at the sky for the stars, but for her brothers. She had a good view of the Bolchet V colony from the observatory.

As painful as it was to think of them in the mines, she wanted to look at the colony while she told them that she'd not fail them. She'd pass her exams and earn enough money to get them out of there. She had to. Very few people lasted long on Bolchet V.

As Claudia shuffled past, she felt her instructor's hand on her arm. "If it helps," Matron said, her voice soft, almost caring, "do well on your testing, and you can visit the stars." Claudia sensed she'd been gifted a rare glimpse at a crack in Matron's hard-as-chromium persona. "But you won't get anything close to that if your scores aren't in the top three of Psi Testing this afternoon. I suggest you eat something and then practice."

THE CAFETERIA TEEMED with tables filled with psi-candidates all dressed in their white jumpsuit uniforms. The room buzzed with nervous energy. A third of them faced testing today.

Claudia went through the line and grabbed as much food as she thought she could hold down. The food at the university was great, most of it made from real ingredients instead of synthetics.

If this was her last chance to eat real food, she might as well make the most of it. By the time she left the line, she had a pile of bacon, eggs, and a variety of fruits that rose so high she had to walk carefully so it wouldn't topple. The smoky scent of the bacon made her mouth water.

Getting a place here was like winning the lottery for someone in her family's rankings. They had no money to buy an apprenticeship. If she hadn't tested as having Psionic potential, she'd be working an unskilled job like her brothers.

Living an existence where success was defined by surviving to the next day.

She'd just gotten to her seat when Grieg slid in beside her. His tray had a respectably normal amount of food on it. But then again, his family was rich, and they could get real food any time he wanted.

"Morning," Grieg said looking down at her tray with amusement. "Got enough food there, Cod?"

"Will you please stop calling me that?" Claudia said.

"Sorry, Cod, but that's what your initials spell. It must be used."

"You're just saying that because your initials spell god and you want everyone to call you that."

Despite the name thing, it was hard to get mad at Grieg, and it wasn't just because of his cheekbones and dark curly hair. He was genuinely nice to everyone, regardless of their family rankings, even those most people ignored, like herself.

"You could just call me Claudia and then I wouldn't want to punch you."

He pointed to her overflowing plate. "That anger is likely from hunger. You should eat more."

She smirked at him and shoveled a forkful of eggs into her mouth.

"Oh," Grieg said, pulling a small package out of his uniform pocket. I was picking up a package from my family and saw this for you."

Claudia's eyes widened. "Really? Thanks!" She never got packages. It was from her brothers. This must have cost them all their spending money.

Grieg cleared his throat awkwardly. "The address said Bolchet V. That's not where your brothers are, is it?"

While she'd told Grieg her family was depending on her to earn enough to buy her brothers an apprenticeship, she hadn't told him where they were. The death rate in the mining colony was 50%, mostly from lung rot—a horrific death. She already felt enough like the pity friend.

"It is, but not for much longer. I'm getting them out. Remember?"

Grieg looked at her with sadness, but said, "Yes you are."

She tore open the package. Inside were two small geometrically designed pendants. Her brothers must have made them out of scrap metal, each one had lines and curves in no logical pattern that she could discern. It was almost as if they'd made something together, warped it, and then broken it in half.

The gift puzzled her. Normally, her brothers had a knack for getting her something she really needed before she even knew she needed it. But, two pendants? That did not seem practical in any way.

Beneath the pendants were two small pieces of wire and a note. She rolled her eyes. Her brothers thought wire was an essential supply. She opened the note.

Hey Sis,

We believe in you. Good luck on your testing.

Mom and Dad say Hi.

We hope you like your pendants. Don't throw away the wire even though we know you want to.

Love you,

Dave & Drew

Grieg looked over at the note, then looked at the gift. "Those are cool. What are you going to do with them?"

Claudia thought for a minute and then smiled. She'd get to thank her brothers and tell them that she actually used the wire. Claudia wrapped a piece of wire into each pendant and then attached them to her boot zippers.

The boots had been a parting gift from her parents who

wanted to make sure her feet would be warm no matter what climate she ended up in. With the pendants on them, it would be like having all of her family near her. Again, her brothers found the perfect gift.

Just as she finished attaching the second pendant, an alarm sounded. Necks at every table craned trying to figure out what was going on.

"Is this part of our testing?" Claudia asked.

"Beats me."

Matron walked through the door, followed by two people, a male and female, in black uniforms and nisstar capes. The capes' fabric shimmered in a way that played tricks with the surrounding light, at times making them look like they'd disappeared. Fearful murmurs echoed around them.

Claudia instantly recognized the pair as part of the Psion Collective and nervous sweat ran down her back. "Are we being tested by actual members of the collective? I thought it was just our instructors."

"I don't think so," Grieg said, then leaned in and whispered. "They've got khodoos."

Claudia shifted her gaze to their waists and winced at the sight of the silver whips at their sides. These were used on criminals. Once they were around you, tiny needles burrowed into your skin ensuring you would be no trouble. If you decided to try anyway, with a push of a button, they could send enough volts through your system to make you quickly change your mind.

Though she'd done nothing wrong, Claudia found herself wishing she could disappear behind a nisstar cape herself. The last thing she wanted to risk was drawing their attention to her. The Psi Guards were not known for their empathy. Ironic, given that they could read your thoughts. She'd make it a point to use her gifts differently whenever it was her turn to serve in the guard. Provided she passed, of course.

Matron's face was drawn tight as she scanned the room.

"Settle down," she said, the strain obvious in her voice. "I need to see Daniel Everheart and Bethan Wahler."

All eyes turned to see the two young men stand up, their faces drained of color. They both walked slowly forward, eyes resolute and fixed on Matron. About a third of the way there, Daniel spun and ran full speed toward another exit. Bethan instantly threw his hands up so they'd know he was not resisting.

The female guard grabbed Bethan and bound his hands, while the other sprinted after Daniel. The woman's hair was sleek, blond, and cut in a sharp bob.

The room was silent as the Psion marched Bethan toward the front. Just as they reached the table where Claudia sat, the woman stopped. She turned, then narrowed her eyes, studying Claudia. Without thinking, Claudia grabbed Grieg's hand, grateful he didn't pull away.

Even though the guard had not laid a finger on her, Claudia had the distinct impression the Psion had read something that Claudia didn't even know about herself. Slowly, the woman turned away and walked out the door with her prisoner.

Grieg looked at Claudia. "Did she read you?"

"Not a clue, and something tells me it would be best if I never found out." Claudia pushed her plate aside no longer hungry.

As soon as the Psion's left, Matron called everyone to attention. "This morning's incident has required a change of scheduling. You are all to proceed to the assembly room. Before your examinations begin, we will bear witness to a Gal-ui Examination."

The hair on Claudia's arm stood up. She'd heard of these interrogations, of course, but didn't know anyone who'd actually attended one. Her father used to run freight before his illness. Stories were whispered about them in dark taverns on every planet in the system. They were said to be a death sentence for those who didn't cooperate. She felt a bit ashamed of herself for being excited about the prospect of getting to witness one. She didn't want anyone to die. She just wanted to know what actually happened at one.

CLAUDIA AND GRIEG made their way down the rows of silver chairs. The telescreens that covered the walls of the room, normally decorative or filled with images of their most prestigious graduates, were now black. It gave the room an oppressive feel, like the walls were closing in on them.

The two members of the Psion Collective sat behind a table on the stage. Daniel was brought in first and seated in a chair in front of the table, but facing toward the spectators. His hands were bound behind him, an unnecessary precaution. The red blotches on his skin clearly showed they'd deployed their khodoos. Bethan was brought in next, also seated with his hands bound. She couldn't imagine what two students could have done to require a Gal-ui. Those types of interrogations were reserved for the most dangerous suspects.

The male Psion stood up and came to the center of the stage. He was of average height, but his bearing held a confidence that made him seem taller and not someone to be messed with, even if he weren't a Psion.

He addressed the students. "While some of you may have developed your abilities enough to read the interrogation, I would like to remind you that doing so is a crime. No matter how tempted you are, I recommend against it. Believe me, we will know."

Claudia shifted uneasily in her chair. She leaned back and concentrated, creating a wall in her mind. The last thing she wanted to do was accidentally make a read. Getting arrested would not save her family.

The man moved back behind the table. Next, the female Psion, who had stared at Claudia, stood up and walked around the table. She placed herself between the two young men.

"You know why you're here. You know what information we want. Make it easy on yourselves. We'll get the information either way."

Bethan's face looked resigned. There was little chance he'd resist. Daniel was a different story. His jaw clenched. Face defiant.

She leaned over and whispered to Grieg. "Why are they letting us watch this? Aren't these normally done in private?"

Grieg tightened his lips briefly, a habit Claudia knew meant he was thinking. "I think it's a warning."

"A warning for what?"

"Loyalty," Grieg said quietly.

His answer made Claudia feel a bit naïve. Why wouldn't they be loyal? Weren't the Psions there for the service of humanity? She should have paid better attention to politics, but her parents had always said it wouldn't matter. They had no influence, so why stress? But, as a Psion, she'd be assisting the rulers. She made a mental note to try and catch up.

The woman walked behind Bethan, her movements as precise as her bobbed haircut. Before she even put a hand on him, Bethan started to convulse. A blue foam bubbled from his mouth.

A suicide tablet! Claudia gripped her seat.

His body slid off his chair in fits. Medics rushed in, but it wouldn't matter. He'd be dead before they got him from the stage.

What could a student possibly know that would be worth dying to hide?

Without any indication that the death of a young person mattered, the woman turned her attention to Daniel. His face hardened.

The interrogation went on silently for about thirty seconds. Daniel's face grew more strained as he resisted the Psion. His body trembled with effort. He wouldn't last much longer like this.

"Just tell them," Claudia whispered, desperately hoping not to see the result of his refusal.

In a burst of will Daniel shouted out, "Vivat resistentia!"

The male Psion shouted, "Finish him."

Claudia resisted the urge to bring down the wall she'd built in her mind. She barely knew Bethan and Daniel. They were good students but had always been quiet and kept to themselves.

The male Psion stormed from his seat and put both hands on Daniels head. She heard Grieg gasp next to her but was too invested in watching to ask why. Daniel let out an agonizing scream she would never forget, then his body went slack.

The female Psion, fury evident on her face, snapped at her counterpart, "I could have gotten the information. Now we'll never have it."

Claudia looked at Grieg and whispered, "Was he just...? She couldn't bring herself to say it."

The color had drained from Grieg's face. "Shattered? Yes. He'll live out his days in insanity as a vegetable."

Claudia felt her breakfast begin to rise from her stomach and now wished she had not eaten so much. She tried to hop up and rush to the bathroom, but Grieg threw his arm in front of her keeping her locked in her seat.

"Don't draw attention to yourself," he said. There was an urgency in his voice.

Claudia's throat burned as she forced the food back down with a swallow and willed it to stay there.

Like Bethan, Daniel was removed from the stage by the medics. Never had the assembly room been this quiet.

Matron walked to the stage as the Psions positioned themselves at the two exits. Voice tight, she said, "I'd like all students to return to their rooms in an orderly fashion."

Claudia intentionally steered herself away from the exit where the male Psion stood. He frightened her. All she wanted to do was get to her room where she'd feel safe. As Grieg and Claudia walked through the other exit, the female Psion grabbed her arm.

"Come with me," the woman said.

Claudia tensed and looked around in panic. "I didn't read anything. I promise. I didn't."

Her classmates refused to meet her eyes, including Grieg. The Psion did not respond as she yanked Claudia out of line.

THE PSION MARCHED Claudia through a series of underground tunnels. The metallic walls held no clues as to location or direction. There were no labels anywhere. It was like walking through the inside of a giant metallic snake.

Between the fast pace they kept and Claudia's constant protests that she had not read anything, she was starting to struggle to get a breath. Not that it mattered. If it weren't for the fact that the woman had her grip firmly on Claudia's arm, she'd think the Psion did not even know she was there.

The tunnel ended abruptly. When the Psion placed her hand on the metal in front of them, it split apart like a door with a whooshing sound and the slight scent of ozone. It opened onto a landing port. A man in plain gray clothes rushed over to them. His eyes flicked over to Claudia and then back to the woman. You could see the question in his eyes, though he said nothing.

"Get her in," the Psion said.

The man took Claudia's arm and obeyed without question. They were putting her on a space shuttle.

They were bringing her off world.

She had no clothes. No way of contacting anyone. She'd also not get to take her exams, which meant her brothers would be condemned to the mines. She couldn't let that happen.

"Please, tell me what's going on. I beg you. I didn't read the interrogation. I swear." She'd briefly considered trying to run but had seen firsthand how hopeless that would be.

Neither of her captors said a word.

This was her first time on a private shuttle. There were six beige colored leather seats, including the ones for the pilot and co-pilot. It was much cleaner than public transport.

The man pulled out a tablet and did a quick scan. "The mind weave is still intact."

Mind weave? Claudia had read about those. Only the best of the best Psions could create one. Not only could they block any attempt at reading, but if by some genius level of skill someone managed to break through, the thoughts of the people inside the weave would give false information that, even to a Psion, would ring true. Why would they need one for their shuttle?

The woman nodded, then said. "Daniel is shattered and Bethan blue-pilled."

The man flopped into one of the chairs. "I'm sorry."

"We all know the risks," she said without a trace of feeling.

The man glanced at Claudia. "The girl?"

The Psion indicated for Claudia to sit down and then held out her hand.

"I'm Psi Bronwyn. You've probably got questions. I can't answer them yet, but you're not in trouble for anything."

Claudia took her hand and shook it. "You couldn't have

mentioned that at any point you were dragging me through the tunnels?"

"I was busy," she said.

"Yeah... kidnapping is so time consuming," Claudia snapped.

The man in gray tried to hide a smirk.

Psi Bronwyn ignored her comment and moved to the pilot's seat.

"Can I at least know where you're taking me?"

"Best you don't," Bronwyn said.

The man leaned forward and gave Claudia a hypo injection. Before she could protest, her surroundings faded into oblivion.

WHEN CLAUDIA WOKE UP, she was in a dimly lit room that resembled a hospital unit. Beside her glowed a console that displayed information about her vitals. There were several other beds nearby, all empty.

Thankfully, she wasn't restrained. Claudia slowly sat up and slid down from the bed.

A woman in a red Lycra medical uniform walked in. "Ah, you're awake. Stay put." The med tech left the room and returned a few minutes later with Psi Bronwyn, who looked absolutely exhausted.

The Psion looked Claudia over for a second and said, "Follow me."

"Has anyone ever told you that you're not a great communicator?" Claudia asked as she tried to keep up with Psi Bronwyn.

They walked through multiple nondescript cream-colored hallways filled with doors labeled with letters and numbers but nothing else to tell you what they were for. Psi Bronwyn stopped at L-24 and pressed a button.

The door slid open. There were two other people in the room sitting at a small round table, one of whom was the man who injected her. The other was an older man, maybe mid-fifties. Other than the table, the room was sparse with a smart screen on one wall and a plant on a stand against another.

"Have a seat," Psi Bronwyn said.

Claudia chose one as far away from injecto-man as she could.

Psi Bronwyn introduced Claudia to the others. Injecto-man was called Psi Benjamin. The older man was Psi Waylen. Bronwyn pushed a button on the table and Claudia's file appeared on the screen, including pictures of her family.

Her stomach clenched.

Psi Bronwyn turned to face her. "What did you think of the shattering?"

Daniel's scream involuntarily rose in Claudia's mind, and she saw his body slump to the ground, mouth slack. "I thought it unjust and cruel."

"And if I told you that the student was a serious threat to the security of the government, would you still think that?" Bronwyn asked.

"I would think our government can't be that powerful if two young men, who haven't even graduated the academy, were such a threat." Claudia said.

"You would be wrong," Psi Benjamin said. "Our government—"

Psi Bronwyn held up her hand and Benjamin went silent. "I will say that I am sympathetic to your views on shattering. In fact, I have a theory that they can be healed, and I want you to help me do it."

Claudia stared at them blankly, thoroughly confused. Finally, she responded with the brilliant retort, "What?"

"We think you can heal the shattered," Benjamin said. "I know you have no reason to trust us, but believe me when I tell you we're the good guys."

"I don't believe you," Claudia said. "Good guys don't kidnap and drug people. They talk to them. Besides, I'm just a student. Sure, my grades are good, but you guys are far more advanced. You wouldn't need me."

"That's where you're wrong," Waylen said. He motioned for Bronwyn to say something.

"I am one of the most skilled Psions currently serving," Bronwyn said in a tone that clearly indicated she wasn't used to having to explain her actions. "I also have a unique gift. One that allows me to read not only the potential of other Psions, but their character. I've been looking for a very particular skill set coupled with an equally specific ethos. I've found some with all the skills, but lacking the right character. Others have had the character but lacked the skills. You're one of the first with everything I need."

"One of the first," Claudia said. "Where are the others?"

It did not shock Claudia in the least when Psi Bronwyn ignored her question and instead asked her own. "Are you willing to help us?"

The idea of healing those who were shattered was appealing, but she didn't exactly trust this group. Besides, what could she actually do? Potential is one thing, but she was still just a student, nothing compared to the Psions surrounding her.

When Claudia didn't answer right away, Waylen said, "Do you understand what happens to the shattered?"

"It means they're in a vegetative state," Claudia said.

Waylen shook his head, indicating she got it wrong. "That's only part of it. Yes, they're in a vegetative state and can't move, but their minds are going all the time. We call it shattered because every memory they have is broken into pieces. They're lost in a maze of broken bits of memory they can't place. It's like you're trapped in your own personal horror film, and it goes on for eternity."

Claudia felt light-headed. The thought of her classmate like that...of anyone like that...

"I just don't think I can do something you can't," she said to them.

"And I say you can," Bronwyn replied.

"Okay, let's say I help you. Does that mean you'll call my family and let them know I'm okay? Though, I do need to take my exams first. It's really important."

"I'm afraid that is no longer possible. As soon as we brought you here, they were sent a notice that you have withdrawn."

Claudia shook her head. "No, no, no. You can't do that. My family is counting on me. I *have to* graduate." Her eyes started to burn as unbidden tears threatened to betray her. She blinked them away, unwilling to give them the satisfaction. "You have no right to do that! It's a lie. It's wrong!"

"You'll find a lot about life is like that," Benjamin said quietly.

"And if I refuse?"

"We'll modify your memory and send you home."

"How about option three where I say no, and you return me to school with my brain completely untouched, telling them there was a miscommunication and I didn't withdraw?"

Waylen chuckled. "I like her."

"This is bigger than you," Bronwyn said.

"I'm not worried about me. I'm worried about my family."

Bronwyn rolled her eyes. "There are things that are bigger and more important than one family,"

"Then fill me in."

"Frankly, there isn't time, and you wouldn't understand half of it."

Claudia needed to think. Empathy was obviously not Bronwyn's strong suit. She needed leverage.

"Well, I'm not as stupid as you think. In fact, I'm smart enough to realize that if it is that big of a deal, then you need me," Claudia said.

"No one is calling you stupid," Waylen said. "What Bronwyn would have said, if she had a bit more tact, is that a lot of it has to do with the inner workings of galactic politics, along with some Psionic theory that you are completely in the dark about and we're on a timeframe that does not give us the luxury of adding that to what you need to learn."

Claudia considered what he said. She was honest enough with herself to realize there were many things she'd not been taught. She definitely didn't understand politics either. Her last conversation with Grieg had made her ignorance abundantly clear.

"Fine," she said after a few moments. "But you have to get my brothers off the Bolchet V Colony AND get them a decent apprenticeship. Otherwise, you can just go ahead and modify my memory and start your search over for another student to kidnap and traumatize." Claudia folded her arms and sat back, trying not to look worried that they'd call her bluff.

Bronwyn smirked. "If you want to prove to me that you're that smart, you may want to start by remembering that I am one of the most powerful readers around."

Claudia deflated a little. She didn't even try to put up a wall around her mind. *Stupid. Stupid. Stupid.* It's the first thing she should have done. That's Psion Defense 101.

"However," Bronwyn said, her voice softening a little, "if you manage to actually heal the shattered, I'll make sure your brothers are safely placed in an apprenticeship. But only if you succeed. Fail, and I can drop you off to work the mines with them."

"Yeah," Claudia said. "You're the good guys."

Before assigning her quarters, they gave her a tablet filled with theory to study. Even though she only got a couple of hours of sleep, she didn't get through the entire tablet, and only understood about half of what she did read.

A chirp at her door signaled someone was there. She pressed the button to open it, and Benjamin stood in the hallway with a stupid grin on his face. Instead of the plain gray clothes he had worn when she first met him, he wore denim jeans and a t-shirt that read, *Off worlders do it better,* and had a rather X-rated image on it.

"Classy," Claudia said.

Benjamin looked offended. "What? I thought you'd find me less intimidating this way. They want me to bring you to breakfast."

"If it's okay with you, I'd rather be led by someone who hasn't drugged me, especially one wearing a perv shirt."

"Hey," Benjamin said raising his hands up innocently. "I only drug people when ordered."

Claudia tilted her head and made a face. "Oh, that solves everything then. Fine. Let's go."

The room they entered felt more like a restaurant than a cafeteria. The tables were round and had padded chairs around them. There were a lot more people in the same plain gray clothes that Benjamin had worn the day he met her and a few in Psion uniforms. She hadn't seen any windows, so Claudia had no idea if she was on a planet or a ship. There was probably no point in her asking either.

The conversations died when people realized Claudia had walked in.

"Super. I'm the freak."

Benjamin put a hand on her shoulder, causing Claudia to jump. "No drugs. Just trying to be reassuring." He leaned in and whispered, "Just so you know. You're not the freak. You're the hope."

Great. First her family's only hope, now a room full of strangers. Having potential really sucked sometimes.

They sat down at a table with Bronwyn and Waylen. There was a plate ready for her, loaded with all her favorite foods.

"Wow, my file is thorough."

"Darn skippy, it is," said Waylen. "Do you think we let anyone in the cool kid's club?

"Darn skippy?" Claudia laughed and chomped down on a piece of bacon. "What century were you born in?"

They gave her enough time to finish her breakfast before Bronwyn sat back and asked her what she'd learned from her reading.

"Well," Claudia said, wiping her mouth with a napkin. "The theory is I read their minds and try to entice the pieces back together. Did I get that right?"

"Close," Waylen said. "Your consciousness has to actually go into their mind. Then, you have to find which of the shattered pieces fit together and try to make them whole. Like a giant puzzle."

"That sounds...absolutely impossible."

"Hey," Benjamin said. "If it were easy, we wouldn't have scoured half the galaxy trying to find the right person.

"How in the world do you expect my consciousness to get inside someone's head?"

A voice sounded from behind her. "That's where I come in."

Claudia turned around to see the oldest looking man she'd ever seen in her life. His face was fairly smooth for an old guy, but his neck looked like a giant, pale raisin. His hair was gray and buzzed close to his scalp. Even though he looked like he could topple over at any moment, his countenance held the confidence of someone whose skills were in high demand. That's when she noticed the black cables snaked around his legs.

He followed her gaze. "These are my stabilizers."

"Claudia, meet Methuselah," Benjamin said.

Claudia held out her hand. "Nice to meet you, Methu—"

The table started laughing. It was the first time Claudia had seen Bronwyn laugh. It made her look almost...nice.

"His name is Carl," Bronwyn said. "That's Benjamin's idea of a joke. You know? Methuselah. The man from ancient Earth that lived longer than anyone else."

"Ah, yes, so funny," Carl said. "I'd beat you with my cane if I had one." He turned to Claudia. "We've got some work to do. Finish breakfast, then meet me in the gym."

He turned and walked away with silent steps as his stabilizers controlled his legs.

THE GYM TURNED out to be a small empty room with two chairs, a small table off to the side, and a nutrition dispenser.

"When you said gym, I thought there'd at least be weights or a mat," Claudia said.

"Oh, don't worry, you'll get a great workout." He pointed to one of the chairs for her to sit. "I've seen your reading scores. You're good, but you'll need to be phenomenal. And we need to add to your skillset."

Claudia rubbed her thumb and index finger together nervously as she thought about having to enter someone's consciousness. "How do we do that?"

"Well, we'll start easy. We won't jump right into a shattered mind, just an old one. I'd like you to not just read me but join me."

"I just don't understand what the joining is."

Carl walked over to the nutrition dispenser and got two bottles of water. He handed one to Claudia. "It means you don't just read their thoughts, you become part of them. Our theory is by doing this you can start to put the shattered pieces of a mind back together."

Claudia took a sip of water. "You see, it's the word 'theory' that has me worried. That means no one has been able to do it."

Carl hesitated, giving her the distinct feeling that he was warring with himself about how much to say. "We've come close," he finally said.

Something about the way he said that made her nervous. "What went wrong?"

"We didn't factor their insanity in, nor that they would fight the joiner."

The hairs on the back of Claudia's neck stood up. "What happened to the person who was in there?"

Carl's whole demeanor changed. His lips tightened into a line and his eyes went from sad to resolved. "They were shattered." His voice was strained as he said it.

Claudia's eyes went wide. No one ever mentioned she'd be in danger.

"Don't worry," Carl said. "We regrouped, thoroughly studied what happened and discovered we needed a different mix of skills to deal with someone in that state. You have those skills. But we don't want you going in unprepared."

The prospect of being shattered was worse than being killed. End her life, fine. Lose her mind, no thanks. Maybe she should just have them adjust her memories and be done with this whole thing.

But, if she ran away, she'd be safe while her brothers would be condemned to a half-life in the mines. She'd never be able to live with herself.

She took a deep breath. "What do I need to learn?"

Carl smiled. "You'll start by joining me. I'm a harmless old man. Nothing to worry about."

"Except, I've never learned anything at school about joining," Claudia pointed out.

Carl sat down in one of the chairs. "Maybe interrupt less and I can tell you how."

"Fine. Shutting up. Teach away."

"When you read me, I want you to block out everything but what you see in my mind. Then, picture yourself there."

He held out his hand. His knuckles looked as gnarled as the roots of an old tree. Methuselah. Claudia took his hand gently, afraid of hurting him, and focused. His thoughts opened readily. She saw a muscular, attractive young man with thick dark hair that he wore down to his shoulders, standing in a field. She instinctively knew this was a younger version of Carl. It felt a little creepy that she thought of him as hot. She tried to shake the thought and attempted to picture him as he was.

Carl slapped her hand gently. "Don't try to change my persona. You're supposed to join it."

"But, I thought it would be you now, not—"

"I got news for you kid. All us old folks, we still see ourselves young. Try not to get distracted by how gorgeous I am."

"Gross," Claudia said, but her face grew warm. She really hoped Carl didn't notice.

She focused only on his thoughts.

"Good," Carl said. "Now, tune everything else out and join me. Notice where I am."

Claudia created a wall around anything else that could leak into her consciousness so she could focus. Then, she pictured herself standing there with him. The next thing she knew, she found herself in the field. Carl turned toward her and smiled.

Then, he walked over and kicked her in the stomach.

Claudia felt herself being torn out of his mind, like being pulled down a wind tunnel. She doubled over.

She felt that kick. Like really felt it.

"When you said they fought back, I didn't think you meant like literally fought. Did you have to kick me?"

"A man's got to use his legs when he can. What? You can't even beat an old cripple?"

Claudia straightened herself up. "Oh, game on, old man."

They went back and forth for hours. Claudia would get in, make a bit of progress, then he'd boot her out. Each time grew a bit more painful.

She sat in one of the chairs out of breath. A bead of sweat ran down her forehead. "Why does it feel so..."

"Physical?" Carl finished for her.

Claudia nodded and wiped her brow with the back of her sleeve. "It's like my body is working out with my mind."

"It is. Our brains are marvelous. We can convince ourselves something is happening to us in a way that makes our bodies respond as if it really is. I have a dream of being able to workout while sleeping, but I haven't gotten it to work yet."

"That would be nice," Claudia said after taking a sip of water.

Carl patted her on the shoulder. "You're doing better than expected this early..."

"I sense a *but*," Claudia said, rubbing her fingers again.

"They won't fight back straight on, like I am. We discovered some of them will use psychological tactics. They can create nightmarish scenarios. Remind yourself that if they can create something in their mind, so can you. Use that to fight back. That's what we'll do next."

"Is it wrong I'm mildly interested to see what you come up with?"

Carl laughed. "I knew you'd grow attracted to this smoking hot mind at some point. You're only human."

Claudia snorted and water came out of her nose, causing her to choke a little.

Some chirps at the door rang out.

"Enter," Carl said.

Bronwyn walked in. "I see you two are working hard. We need to talk. Bring Claudia."

Carl tossed Claudia a small towel to wipe her face. "I guess we'll get some lunch."

THEY DIDN'T EAT in the common area this time, but in Bronwyn's quarters. Claudia had expected a 'necessities only' type of room, but it was surprisingly decorative. There were beautiful paintings of seasides, ceramic models of ancient lighthouses, and seashells arranged artfully around the room.

Everyone but Benjamin sat down at a wide dining table. Claudia heard someone knocking around in a separate part of the quarters, along with some sizzling and the smell of garlic.

That's when Benjamin appeared with plates in his hand. When he put them on the table, Claudia's mouth started to water. "Is that..."

"Seafood alfredo," Benjamin finished for her. "I'd saved up for a while to get these ingredients shipped. I was going to use them on a hot date tonight, but—"

"But, no one is going to have free time for a while," Bronwyn said. "Waylen's got some news. Let's get some food and then we'll get into what he's learned."

Everyone filled their plates. Claudia watched carefully to see how much they loaded onto theirs before getting her own. It was one thing to be a bit greedy at school, but she didn't want to embarrass herself in front of this group.

She took a bite. Her eyes widened at the salty buttered taste of the parmesan combined with the umami of the seafood. "Oh, my goodness." She didn't care that the others were looking at her amused. Claudia shoved another bite in her mouth and savored it, then looked at Benjamin. "This is the best thing I've ever eaten in my life."

He stood up and took a bow.

After giving everyone a few minutes to enjoy their food, Waylen pushed his empty plate toward the center of the table and took a deep breath. "I've heard from my contact. We have two pieces of bad news. They've begun replacing instructors at all the Earth schools. With sympathetics."

The atmosphere around the table tensed, but Claudia wasn't sure why. "Can someone tell me what that means?"

Bronwyn tucked some of her hair behind her ear and put her fork down. "There is a faction in the Collective that believes it should be Psions running the government and not merely aiding those who rule. About a year ago, we realized it was becoming a plan instead of just wishful thinking."

"In case you're not sure why that's a bad thing," Benjamin said, "it would be too much power in the hands of people who already have a natural hands up. Plus, other planets have tried it. Universally, it ended up in totalitarianism."

"What do the schools have to do with that?" Claudia asked.

Carl finished his bite and said, "Answer this. If you want to take over a group of people, but do not have the raw power to overthrow them, what strategy could you employ to take over without even having to fight?"

Claudia wasn't sure what conclusion he wanted her to reach, but it obviously had something to do with the schools. That's when it hit her. "Convince the upcoming generation that they'd be better off with Psions in charge."

Carl smiled. "Got it in one."

"We need to move up the timeline," Bronwyn said. "The evidence we need is in one of the shattered. From what Waylen has learned, they've put Psions with suggestive capabilities in every school on Earth. They're going to move quickly, and we need to be ready."

She looked at Claudia and continued. "Here's where you come in. We have some people undercover whose job was to find out who the main players are and how far up the Psion organization this plot goes. We know they've learned something important. We received a message saying they had the evidence we needed, but the person who had it was shattered before he could get us the information. We need you to try and restore him so he can tell us what he knows."

"She needs more training," Carl said. "We haven't even started on psychological defenses yet."

"I'm not sure we have the time to wait," Waylen said.

"They're not going to take over in the next few weeks," Carl argued. "It will take them a few years to build the support they need."

"Wait," Claudia said. "You mentioned two pieces of bad news."

Bronwyn took a deep breath and said, "The person they shattered was Psi Garrison."

Claudia didn't know who he was, but the pronouncement sucked the air out of the room.

"He's the only one who knew our names," Benjamin said, looking at Claudia. "We lead the opposition. We suspect they may have gotten that information from him. Which means if we don't get the evidence soon, they're going to be able to track us down and then there won't be any way to stop them."

Claudia looked at the group around her. They were risking their lives to stop their own kind from gaining power because they thought it would harm people. They'd also gone through a lot of trouble to find a way to heal the shattered.

Doing that weakened their leverage against people. Even if she couldn't think of them as the good guys yet, they were definitely better than the other guys. She stood up. "I'm willing to try."

Benjamin piled another serving of seafood alfredo on her plate. "Eat some more first. You'll need the energy."

THEY WHEELED in Psi Garrison on a medical bed. He looked frozen. Claudia had thought the shattered would look more... insane? Certainly not this placid. What surprised her more than that was how young he looked. He must still be in his twenties. He had sandy blond hair cut short, and brown eyes. His eyes were wide open but showed no signs of life.

She placed a hand on him gently trying to imagine what was going on in his mind. The weight of what she was trying to do and just how unprepared she really was pressed in on her. Her chest tightened.

Carl stood beside her. "He already feels threatened and doesn't know you. There's a symbol that you can share with him to show you're safe. It's a way our group has of identifying themselves to one another. I don't know if he'll interpret it correctly, but try." Carl closed his eyes and sent her the symbol.

"A bridge? Wait. I've seen this somewhere."

"It's the Unity Bridge," Carl said. "Get that picture firmly in your mind. He may be more willing to let you work with him. Try to fit some pieces together. Our theory is the more you can fit together, the more his sanity will return."

Claudia nodded and said, "I'm ready." Then she took a deep breath hoping it was true.

She probed Psi Garrison's mind to try to get a read on him. Most minds felt cloudy and cool, but his was sharp. Claudia sucked in a breath. Tiny pieces of broken glass swirled. They literally meant *shattered*. How could she join him without getting sliced to bits? Even just trying to get a read felt like she was running through razors.

Think. Claudia imagined an invisible shield going up around her body. Slowly, the scratches eased, but she still couldn't see Psi Garrison. Could she join him when he wasn't in her vision?

She had to get in there somehow, so she pictured herself floating amidst the shards. As she entered, the shards pressed against her shield in rapid thrusts, but it held.

She called out to him. "Psi Garrison!"

Something rushed her from behind and pushed. "Go away!"

Claudia turned around to see Psi Garrison picking something up to throw at her, his eyes wild with panic.

"I'm safe!" she shouted, trying to show him the bridge; but the moment she projected it shards of glass sliced through the image warping it as it floated away.

"Leave me alone!" he screamed. She barely had time to duck as a giant rock came at her.

"Look, I'm safe." She projected the bridge's image again, but the same thing happened. Throwing up her hands, she tried to grab at the broken pieces of the bridge to put them together. She'd just reached one of them when a loud roar sounded from behind her.

Quickly, she spun around. A massive lion, head down and forward like he was tracking his prey, stalked toward her.

This isn't real. This isn't real. It's just his mind.

Claudia backed up anyway. Carl had told her she could conjure things, too. She pictured a giant stack of meat and hurled it in front of the lion. That worked. The animal started to devour the meat, then disappeared in strands of smoke.

If trying to show Psi Garrison the bridge was not working,

maybe she should focus on trying to put some of his pieces together. She reached out and grabbed a shard, carefully examining it. It reflected Psi Garrison's face, happy and laughing. There was someone else there, but she could only see part of a yellow sleeve.

She grabbed another. This memory was completely different. He was running, looking behind him frantically. A third shard showed something completely different from the first two.

This was impossible. There was no way to get these pieces together in time.

Claudia focused on the happy memory. The yellow sleeve. Shards moved toward her. Another glint of yellow. She grabbed it and put it with the other piece. Another had a shoulder. Now she was getting somewhere.

The air around her heated up and she smelled smoke. Looking around, she saw a fire raging, moving fast in her direction.

Claudia knew it was Psi Garrison's way of keeping her away from the shards. The fire wasn't real. It was his creation. The best thing she could do would be to ignore it and grab the pieces anyway. If she could get a good memory together, it might make him more willing to listen to her.

The flames were almost upon her. She reached out frantically grabbing one shard after another.

Claudia screamed as searing pain ripped through her arm. She pulled it back and saw the burns on her flesh. Something pulled at her like a rope around her waist. A moment later, she was out of Psi Garrison's head and back in the gym, surrounded by the others, the flesh on her hand burning in agony.

Benjamin scooped her up and rushed her to medical. The doctor did a quick scan then carefully wrapped her hand in cellular tape, while someone else injected her with pain reliever. She felt the pain in her hand fade, but it also made her mind a bit fuzzy. There wasn't time for this. While she didn't learn anything important, she could feel Psi Garrison's sense of urgency. Whatever information he had, they needed it fast.

"What happened?" Carl asked her.

"There was a fire, but I thought it was fake, an illusion he created to scare me."

Carl rounded on Bronwyn. "This is why I said she needed more training. There was not enough time for her to absorb everything we'd talked about."

"We have no choice," Bronwyn said. "We could be discovered and silenced at any minute. We have no idea how much they know and who they've taken in. She's our best chance."

"I won't lose another one," Carl said. "Her empathy drives her brain to make it real for her. Awareness needs to be second nature, so she doesn't forget the illusions are a REAL danger."

Claudia held up her wrapped hand. "I'm not likely to forget that now, am I?" She tried to sit up but felt the room spin, so she laid back down.

The med assistant rushed over to her. "You need to rest while the pain meds settle." She lifted Claudia's feet onto the bed and took off her boots. "Your mind will be less fuzzy and back to normal in about 30 minutes."

"I don't want to waste any time," Claudia said.

Bronwyn looked at her. "You won't. Carl, go over everything from the moment she joined. See if we can give her an edge."

Claudia told him everything that happened, moment by moment, while she had been joined with Psi Garrison's mind. He listened without interruption until she finished.

"Did it seem like the bridge image scared him?"

Claudia felt a bit dizzy from the pain meds and laid back for a moment. "Honestly, everything scared him."

"Let's think about this logically," Carl said. "If you're afraid, what you're looking for is safety. What if you—"

"No, wait," Claudia said. "Logic is the problem. The memories were in pieces. Like when you are trying to remember something really important from a dream and only have surreal glimpses that don't make sense. Sort of like how I feel right now. The solution is on the tip of my brain. I know it."

She needed to think but couldn't while just lying there in bed. "I need to walk," Claudia said. "It helps me think. Can you hand me my boots?"

Slipping them on with one hand was no problem. Zipping the left one while twisting her good hand around to do it, however, was a problem. She got the best grip she could on it and yanked. It was a good thing her brothers had made her the pendants.

Then... "The pendants!" Claudia shouted.

"What's wrong?" Carl said, alarmed.

"It's the pendants. That's the solution." She pointed to the gift from her brothers. "Help me get these off my boots."

Once they were off, Claudia held them up. "What does this look like to you?"

"Nothing. Some weird shapes."

"Okay, now imagine your mind is off a bit. Like you're hallucinating."

"Still nothing."

Claudia laughed. "How do my brothers do it? Every single time, they know just what I need." She held up the pendants. "This is how he sees the bridge. This is the Unity Bridge."

Carl tilted his head to look at them from a different angle. "I don't see it."

The trick is to remember he doesn't feel safe. His safety, the Unity Bridge, is broken and warped.

She turned them around each other until she found a way they fit together. "Now look."

Carl smiled.

"Now, get me back to Psi Garrison," she said.

THEY MADE their way back to the gym. Claudia put her burned hand on Psi Garrison's chest and whispered, "I'm going to get your mind back to you."

It was easier to get in the second time, but Psi Garrison was ready. The moment he spotted her, the glass started flying. Claudia threw up a shield around her body.

"Look! Psi Garrison! Look what I have!"

She projected the pendants into his mind, but a glass shard flew through it before he even glimpsed it. She heard deep growls and turned to see a pack of dogs stalking around her.

They're not real. They're not real.

They started barking. She looked down at her wrapped hand. It didn't matter if they were real. They could still hurt her. She conjured another pile of meat, but they didn't give it the least bit of notice. She glimpsed Psi Garrison looking at her from a distance, hiding behind a tree of his own creation. He smiled mischievously. What? Did he create vegetarian dogs?

They don't want meat. Fine. But they probably want to live.

She conjured a pack of coyotes, which chased the dogs away from her.

Claudia hated doing this, but she was going to have to play hard ball. She searched Psi Garrison's emotions for fears.

Broken images of people moved in her direction on the shards of glass, but the people in the image weren't harming him. They were harmed.

He feared for others. These were people he cared about. She searched through the shards, like putting together pieces of a puzzle. Psi Garrison started running toward her, to keep her away from them.

Quickly, she pictured him bound. Long pieces of rope slithered up from the ground, binding him in place, buying her some time. One piece at a time, she found a whole person. It was a little girl, about four years old. Claudia searched for that memory.

Psi Garrison stood on the deck of a starship, looking out at the stars. The little girl stood beside him and listened as he pointed out the different parts of the system they were in. The girl looked enthralled.

Claudia focused on that memory until the little girl stood beside her. Then Claudia pointed to Psi Garrison.

"Daddy!"

Claudia could see the panic in Psi Garrison's eyes, desperate, as he struggled to get out of the ropes.

"Help your daddy," Claudia said holding up the pendants. "Show him these and tell him it is from me."

The little girl walked over to her father. "The lady said to show you this. Why are you in ropes?"

Psi Garrison's eyes softened. He looked back and forth between the pendants and his daughter to Claudia.

Claudia held up her hands. "I'm here to help you. If you'll trust me, we can fix this. I won't hurt your daughter. I won't hurt you. You're safe."

She moved a little closer. When he didn't fight against the ropes, trying to get to her, she released him. He leaned down and grabbed his daughter, holding her close, then picked her up.

"We can fix you. Let's put your memories together."

PIECE BY PIECE, Claudia matched the pieces together as Psi Garrison drew more and more toward her. At first, she worried it would take a lifetime to put all of it together. After all, it was a lifetime's worth of memories. She was relieved to discover that the more they repaired, the faster things came together. Toward the end, decades of thoughts and ideas flowed, finding each other and connecting on their own. His mind started healing itself.

Psi Garrison looked at her and smiled, his daughter still safely in his arms. "You can go now."

Claudia leaned in and booped the little girl's nose and said, "You helped save your daddy." Then, she closed her eyes and allowed herself to drift out of his mind.

When she opened her eyes, she looked down to see Psi Garrison's own eyes, now back to normal. Carl, Benjamin, and Waylen were hugging each other and shouting for joy. Bronwyn nodded appreciatively to Claudia.

Psi Garrison stood up. "I have some important things to tell you."

A WEEK LATER, it was all over the news about the rogue Psions who had planned a government takeover. Bronwyn's rebels were safe.

There was a chirp at Claudia's door. "Enter."

Bronwyn and Carl walked in.

"We intend to keep our part of the deal," Bronwyn said. "We'll get your brothers a great apprenticeship. We have a request, though."

"Okay..."

Carl sat down. "You can go back to school if you'd like, but we'd like to request..." He looked at Bronwyn and then said again, "...*request* that you help us restore others who are shattered."

"I suggested we just kidnap you again and make you do it, but I was outvoted," Bronwyn said.

"I'm a bit uncomfortable that you guys actually vote on things like kidnapping," Claudia said. "But, after what I saw life was like for Psi Garrison, I couldn't live with myself if I didn't help others going through that."

Carl smiled broadly. "I had a feeling you'd say that."

"About my brothers..." Claudia said. She told them about the pendants and her brother's ability to know just what she needed even before she knew. "I have a theory. I believe they have a new type of psionic ability. One we don't know how to recognize yet. That's why I tested for aptitude, but they didn't. I'm also absolutely convinced I'll need them to help the shattered. If they didn't know how the safe image would look to Psi Garrison, I would never have gotten him to trust me. We won't even know what image to use for others. How would you feel about bringing them on board to help?"

"That could work," Carl said.

"It would mean also helping my parents. They won't have my brothers or me to care for them, and they're not doing well as it is."

"I guess now that you've already agreed to help, I can let you in on the strength of your position," Bronwyn said.

"I'm confused. What do you mean?"

"You are the only one who has succeeded in repairing the shattered," Carl said. "Pretty soon, you'll be the most famous Psion around. I wouldn't be surprised if they're writing you into a textbook as we speak."

"Plus," Bronwyn said, "if you're right and it can only be

done in tandem with your brothers, you guys can write your own ticket. Believe me, your family will be well taken care of."

Claudia beamed. "May I send out a few communiques?"

"Of course," Carl said. "Who to?"

"My family, obviously, and—"

Bronwyn smirked, "and some guy named Grieg."

Claudia rolled her eyes. She had to start remembering to put up a wall around her fellow Psions.

INTRODUCTION TO "THE HERESY OF PEACE."

This is one of my favorite stories that I've ever written. It was a combination of two thoughts. I had recently finished reading the book, "The Anatomy of Peace" by the Arbinger Institute for a leadership module I was taking at university. It talks about how we often respond to people in a way that produces the exact opposite results than we want. A few days later, I was thinking about the Black Plague (as one does), but specifically how they tried to solve their problem. At one point, they believed the plague was sent by the devil. Because cats are the devil's familiars, they had a massive program to destroy as many cats as possible. You probably see the problem here. It was the fleas on rats causing the problem and now there weren't enough cats to deal with the rats. The Heresy of Peace asks what if the thing you hate the most is what you need to survive? And what if you're the hated? Would you save your enemy?

4

THE HERESY OF PEACE

It had been three months since the last bombing. The longest between attacks in recent years. Bokrahm would have loved that to mean the d'Nai no longer wanted them dead. He knew better, though.

As he stood on the school stage with his trusty mobile science lab, Bokrahm wiped the sweat pooled between the hard ridges on his forehead. The red sun of Cadesh-shub rose to its pinnacle above the mountain range in the distance. Even through the school's blast mitigation windows, you could see the air's heat undulating in waves.

The children, oblivious to the heat in their excitement, looked up at him with eager faces. After the first presentation he'd done, his daughter, Apa, had warned him that he needed more showmanship. He wouldn't be talking to one of his groups of stuffy committees. Since then, he'd upped his assembly game. This was why he was now surrounded by pink synthetic smoke that irritated his skin. But, it could change colors and make sparks at the press of a button which caused the students to "oooh" so...

The Committee for Scientific Advancement didn't approve of him using his time this way. Their top researcher should be advancing the Nakim's knowledge, not putting on a show for a bunch of kids. They had much less prolific researchers who could wow simple children. But, after Apa died, they gave him leeway. Inspiring the children helped him grieve.

"What color should the smoke be now?" Bokrahm called out.

Every color imaginable was shouted out from the crowd. Every color, except blue, that is. Blue was the color of the d'Nai. It broke his heart how quickly children learned to hate. Were the d'Nai children as averse to the purple color of the Nakim? He'd give anything to see peace in his lifetime.

In just two generations, their nation devolved from an intermingled populace living in harmony, to two segregated groups divided by ideology, hate, and destruction.

"I hear yellow!" Bokrahm said. "But, do you know what? I'm hungry. I think I'll eat some of this pink first. Doesn't it look yummy?"

"Noooo!" the children shouted.

Bokrahm scooped up some of the lingering smoke and brought it to his mouth. He made a yucky face. "Tastes like feet."

"Eeeewww." the children shouted.

His throat caught as he spotted Engriel a few rows back. She was his Apa's best friend. A fever kept her home the day of the bombing. Otherwise...well, he shook the thought away. Today was about entertaining the children while (hopefully) sneaking in some science. "What? You don't like feet? I bet you like Cavern Drops."

The kids shifted in their seats. He had them now. Any adult who gave out Cavern Drops scored an instant jump in the coolness factor. He couldn't blame them. The salted condensation of raspberry-flavored deliciousness was hard to beat. Wait until they learned it was mostly made from fungus. He'd save that bit of scientific knowledge for a colleague to dispense.

"Let's see what I can do here." As Bokrahm turned the smoke dispenser to yellow, sparks popped rapidly. He loved this part and smiled as the children cheered. Bokrahm moved to where he had a beaker simmering. As he lifted the beaker, the doors to the room opened with a bang. The children jumped and nervous screams rang out.

Bokrahm's own heart quickened, but his fears that the d'Nai had attacked the school were allayed when three men in the green uniforms and the gray berets of community guards stormed in and hurried to the stage.

"You're needed, there's been an incident," one of the guards said.

Bokrahm waved a teacher over. "Mix this into the vat I brought. It will create enough Cavern Drops for every child to get one. I'll send someone for my equipment."

The guard looked at the teacher. "Someone will be in touch with updates and when you can release the students."

THEY TOOK him to the forensics building. A knot formed in the pit of his stomach. He hadn't been here since he'd identified his Apa in the morgue. Her broken body no more than an empty shell. Her spirit had moved on to the Ghost Forest.

The guard swiped his card and pushed one of the three unlabeled buttons at the bottom of the selector. So, not the morgue. They were taking him to biocontainment. *Great Architect help us.* What have the d'Nai done now?

As they left the lift, an automated voice instructed them to move to the decontamination chamber. Great. He'd have to strip in front of people. While he was fairly fit for his age, he had aged. A man had his pride, after all.

The guard nodded and left him to enter the chamber alone, a small square room with two doors and frosty colored glass.

Bokrahm placed his clothes in the plastic bag provided for him and stepped under the hoses attached to the ceiling of the chamber. He hated this part. A whoosh sounded as the freezing fluid covered his body. It always left a mild odor of onions on his skin. Couldn't they scent this stuff? Maybe he'd put an intern on that task.

He donned his white protective suit, gloves, and face mask then stepped out the door on the other side. Three bodies, modestly covered with a blanket, were each on an autopsy table. Bokrahm raised his eyebrows in surprise. They were d'Nai bodies.

Their normal blue color was now almost brown. That was unusual. When d'Nai passed, their skin usually dulled to a gray color. He moved closer to get a better look. The men couldn't have been out of their twenties, yet the fur on their arms was thin and brittle.

While the d'Nai did not have the same rituals regarding blood that the Nakim did, it pleased Bokrahm to see whoever did the examinations showed the blood of their enemies respect. A pint of yellow blood from each corpse was carefully contained in a life vessel.

Another doctor in protective gear sat hunched over, looking at the microscope display screen. Only Noam, the head of the research department, had posture that bad.

"Come here and look at this," Noam said without ever looking away from the screen.

Bokrahm looked, then gasped. A gray fetal-like parasite, with antennae appendages had attached to the red blood cells.

"Have you seen that before?" Bokrahm asked.

"No. That's why I sent for you. It's not in any reference material that I could find. From the autopsy, it appears to damage more than the blood cells. I suspect that the appendages are injecting poison. Necrosis spread from the internal organs outward. Only on one of the bodies could it be seen on the surface."

"Maybe the one with the exposed necrosis infected the other two," Bokrahm said. "How widespread is this?"

Noam looked up for the first time. "No idea. These bodies were found just outside the Ghost Forest. "We've isolated the poor woman who found them, and her blood sample showed no sign of infection."

"Why were they near the Ghost Forest to begin with?" Bokrahm asked.

"The security service has been alerted," Noam said. "Three d'Nai on forbidden, religious ground, and now a mysterious illness. We may be facing a bio attack."

TWO DAYS LATER, there were twenty-seven more d'Nai bodies, and Bokrahm sat testifying before The Assembly. Thirty representatives, ten from each of the three castes, sat at desks facing the front of the room where the ruling Twelve sat at the high table observing the proceedings. For the moment, The Twelve were there to listen to and hear the ideas of the representatives. Only after that would they hold their own deliberations and make the big decisions.

Bokrahm sat on the right side of the room, between the representatives and The Twelve, like an intermediary. The press, along with a few Nakim with enough connections to get in, faced him from their seats on the opposite side of the room.

Raised voices were common in assembly chambers. Leading a nation took debate. Some debated a bit louder than others. He didn't mind that. What Bokrahm hated was the grandstanding politicians who only asked questions that promoted their political agenda.

"So, the d'Nai are now attacking us with bioweapons," shouted one assemblyman, a younger member from the military caste trying to make a name for himself. "This is what we get for giving them refuge in our land. They should be expelled!" There were bellows of agreement.

Bokrahm eyed The Twelve to see if they agreed. Their faces remained passive. That was a good sign. In his experience, whenever they leaned toward a decision, their faces became more resolute.

"Well, doctor," the young hotheaded assemblyman said. "Have you determined how they're using this weapon?"

Bokrahm sighed. "Thus far the only ones who've died are d'Nai. If it's a bioweapon, it's not very effective."

"Does ineffective mean there was no plan or just that they were incompetent?" This came from Chazum, one of the few assemblymen he respected. His voice was calm and Bokrahm could tell it was a question born in sincerity.

"That would be a better question for the security group."

Chazum nodded. "Then tell us what you've discovered about the illness."

Finally.

Bokrahm pulled out a data crystal and inserted it in the port in his desk. Holoscreens appeared over each desk.

"As you can see from my summary, the illness is born from a parasite in the blood stream. It injects a substance into the tissue it encounters. We thought the injections were random at first, but we've noticed a pattern. It starts its attack in the extremities. We've gotten to see only four cases in the middle phase, where the d'Nai could still communicate, but not move.

"They'd indicated that it started with numbness in their fingers and feet, then spread from there. As more tissue died, their hearts also started to fail. Death occurs within a few days, but the patient is alert the entire time."

The room was quiet as images showing the different stages of the disease flashed over their holoscreens.

Chazum was the first to speak. "And there have been no cases seen in the Nakim?"

"None," Bokrahm said. "Either we're immune or have not been exposed in a way that transmits the illness. Before you ask, we still don't know how it transmits. Only some of the patients were in contact with one another."

"That you know of," the young assemblymen said. "If they're plotting, they won't tell you everything."

"D'Nai are dying," Bokrahm said. "I suspect they'd prefer I'd find a solution."

Rezule, a representative from the religious caste, stood up. "It appears to me if the d'Nai are the only ones affected, that this is The Great Architect's judgment of them. Are we putting ourselves against The Great Architect by interfering? Maybe we should let their judgment play out its course."

Bokrahm sighed. That didn't take long.

There were murmurs of agreement. A small part of Bokrahm understood their feelings. He'd prayed for judgment from The Great Architect himself when his Apa was first killed. He'd come to see things differently since then, but he was one of the few.

Shandret Olumun, one of The Twelve, stood up, her long gray hair pinned up with elaborate braids. Bokrahm smiled. His wife used to do her hair that way.

It was rare for one of The Twelve to speak during initial testimony and deliberations. Bokrahm remembered Shandret from when she'd come to his home after the bombing that killed Apa. She'd also lost a daughter that day and had come to mourn with him. Something he'd always be grateful for.

"Bokrahm Alters, you have suffered greatly at the hands of the d'Nai, yet still help them. Why?"

The two of them had not met again since their day of mourning, but on that day they burned with enough hatred between them to destroy a world. He could still see the wrath in her eyes, though his had softened.

Bokrahm considered his words carefully. Whatever he said, the three castes would try to interpret in favor of their position.

"It was the Ghost Forests," he said. "I went there often to meditate and, if The Great Architect would allow it, try to gain some wisdom from my ancestors. He did. I expected my wife, but it was Apa's spirit that came. She reminded me that those raised to hate would know nothing else. The killings would never end. Instead, we must give them evidence to counter what they'd been taught. Show them that we do not wish them dead."

"Better them than us," the young assemblyman mumbled.

The murmurs of assent did not bode well for Bokrahm's dream of peace between their peoples. If he didn't find a solution soon, the more militant factions would gain an advantage, and the death toll would rise for both races.

AFTER HIS TESTIMONY, Bokrahm knew he should go back to the lab, but his heart was too heavy with grief. He knew how to heal many illnesses, but angry hearts were beyond his scope. Too bad there wasn't a school for that. Maybe, if he could find a way to cure the d'Nai, it would prove they didn't have to be enemies, but brothers.

When Apa was young, she'd uttered a curse about the d'Nai. Something she'd likely heard at school. Bokrahm did not chasten her. Instead, he grabbed some paint. First, he poured out some blue.

"This the color of d'Nai," he said.

"It's ugly. Just like they are," Apa replied.

Then, Bokrahm picked up some red paint and started mixing it in the blue until it turned the purple of Apa's skin.

"Our color comes from theirs," he said. "We are more alike than you think."

She didn't say anything in reply, but he never heard her utter that curse again. Three weeks later, she was dead from a d'Nai bomb.

What Bokrahm needed now was wisdom to heal both bodies and hearts. He needed to speak with the spirits.

The path leading to the Ghost Forest of Olam brought peace and a feeling of shelter. Tall sweeping trees stood sentinel on either side of the path, while their branches, with feather-like green leaves and gray-blue blossoms, hung to the ground—the combination an example of pride and humility working as one.

Bokrahm reached into his pocket and wrapped his hand around his minchah. He kept the ceremonial knife with him at all times, so he would always be prepared to provide an offering at the Petitioners Altar.

A few moments later, sweeping trees gave way to a different type of forest, one with hollowed out rock formations that whispered in the wind. The greenery and flowers faded to reds and oranges. A desert surrounded by paradise. A gateway to the dead.

In the center stood the Ear of the Architect, a giant, bone smooth circle of mottled stone. Bokrahm pulled out his minchah and made a tiny slice on his palm. He pressed the blood against the stone and walked through the circle onto the narrow petitioner's path. Bokrahm treaded carefully. Only those who stayed on the narrow path had their petitions heard.

A few other Nakim milled about in the hollow. Some just for quiet meditation. Some hoping to hear from their dead. Others, like him, came with a plea in their hearts. Bokrahm went to the sheltered altar where a cedar chest stood to assist the petitioners. He grabbed one of the clean white cloths folded in the drawer of the chest and wrapped his sacrificial wound.

He knelt to pray. "Please, Great Architect, lead us to peace." A large explosion shook the area. Some petitioners screamed. Others wept. Bokrahm braced himself against the ground. Was this The Great Architect's answer? More death? He ran out of the forest and hopped into his transport, hoping the carnage was limited. Smoke and fire rose from the market. He pushed the drive stick down to get there as fast as possible.

A SECURITY TEAM had already started clearing the area. Doctors, medics, and civilians triaged the wounded. The most seriously injured were rushed to the hospital, while the walking wounded were transported to a nearby school which served as an emergency shelter.

Bokrahm would be most useful at the school. A security guard recognized him and helped him push through the crowd. Bokrahm examined one person after another. Some with severe burns. Some with bones protruding. Some already lost. He worked on autopilot setting bones, applying salve, removing shrapnel, and sometimes just covering the body when it was too late. The smell of burned flesh permeated the school. He noticed Noam working with equal fervor.

A young nurse came to him with a soot-covered face, streaked with tears. "I need your help."

Bokrahm followed her to a bed where a young boy, no more than six years old, clung to his father's dead body. His grip was firm, and he screamed any time someone tried to extract him from the corpse. The boy was beyond being reasoned with, and Bokrahm had to call over a few other men to help peel the boy off his father.

Why was this the answer to his prayer?

Fourteen hours of patching people together left Bokrahm barely able to stand. His arms ached and his legs weighed him down so much that he shuffled more than walked.

Noam put a hand on his arm. "You need some rest my friend. You'll do no good if you are making errors from exhaustion."

Bokrahm didn't argue. He followed Noam to a station, where they were given a ride to the hospital. Beds had been set up in the back room for doctors to get a few moments' rest before they would begin another round of holding death at bay. Volunteers walked the room offering food and water.

Bokrahm snatched a bottle of water and drank it greedily. The cool liquid soothed the soreness of his throat, but did not remove the grit from all the smoke he'd inhaled. Even so, it was a balm to his depleted body. At least here, the smell was medicinal and not that of destroyed flesh. He laid down on one of the beds to let his muscles relax. Easing the tension caused its own welcome pain.

Someone turned on the news. Farsal, leader of the d'Nai, was center on the screen. To the Nakim, he was known as Farsal the Butcher. His lies had killed as many as the d'Nai bombs, including those of his own people.

Farsal's blue skin was blotched from rage. The fur on his head and arms grew as wild as his rhetoric.

"The Nakim have tried to kill us with a plague," he

shouted. The large crowd Farsal addressed hissed in anger. "But we are not animals to be put down. Today, we let them know that we will not go down without a fight." Cheers thundered from the crowd. "They accuse us of trying to harm them while secretly releasing this illness on us. None of them are affected by the plague. What does that tell you? Well, today's response will not be the last. We will rid ourselves of the Nakim so we may once again be a free people."

Bokrahm put a pillow over his head to block out the rhetoric and started to roll over, then froze. Neither group would be free like this; not while they'd bound themselves in chains forged by their own hatred.

Farsal's rhetoric would continue whether he listened or not. What he needed to do was find a cure for the d'Nai disease. He had to. Bokrahm pushed himself up, fighting his exhaustion and headed back to the lab. He must find the plague's cause before the d'Nai initiated another attack.

BOKRAHM ASKED the stations to play informational segments over all public holoscreens in the d'Nai areas describing the symptoms and asking people to come to the research center at the first sign of the illness. Unfortunately, Farsal's rhetoric had most of the d'Nai populace believing the Nakim started the illness, which meant they weren't likely to come in for help.

Back at the lab, Bokrahm pulled one of the bodies out of cold storage and put it on the autopsy table. He needed more tissue samples. The ding of a message sounded on his communicator. Bokrahm was grateful he no longer had to wear the complete protective attire. Now that they knew the Nakim were immune, he didn't have to try and juggle the communicator screen with the giant rubber gloves. He was back to his regular old lab gloves.

He pressed a button. "This is Bokrahm."

Noam's face appeared on the screen. "A d'Nai has come in with early symptoms."

"That's incredible! Send whoever it is down here. Can you come too? I have several tests I had planned on the off chance someone actually came. We can work twice as fast."

"I'll be there, along with a whole bunch of security."

"Is that really necessary? I'm sure they've been screened for weapons. How are we to build any peace between one another when we can't trust someone coming for help?"

"Trust me. It's necessary." Noam disconnected the channel without any further explanation.

Bokrahm hurried to move the dead body he was working on back into cold storage to make his d'Nai patient more comfortable. He disinfected the room and had a lab tech bring in an actual bed instead of just an autopsy table. He'd just spread clean sheets on it when his patient walked in.

Bokrahm couldn't trust his own eyes. "Is that—"

"Farsal Bgnei," Noam said. "Yes, it is. A bit hypocritical but we'll take him anyway."

"Taking is all you know how to do, isn't it?" Farsal said to Noam.

"And this is his son, Kemel," Noam said ignoring the comment as he pointed to young man in his twenties. Kemel was fit, had a strong jawline, intelligent blue eyes that matched his skin, and head and arms full of black fur. He was the exact opposite of his father who had pasty blue skin, a gut that said he enjoyed more food than was needed for sustenance, eyes as dark as his soul, a receding chin, and a balding head.

Bokrahm could only hope their ideologies were as different as their appearance.

Farsal turned to Bokrahm. "You may take my blood to run

your tests, but do not touch me with your skin. I require you to wear gloves at all times."

"That's not an issue," Bokrahm said. "Have a seat on this bed. Step one is to see if you're actually infected."

After Bokrahm drew some blood, he put it in the analyzer. Noam met him at the machine.

"Be careful here, friend," Noam said. "I know you want to build a bridge with the d'Nai, but I fear this one is booby trapped. He's up to something."

"You are probably right, but my job is to heal. I'll watch my back. I promise."

"And your front and sides as well, please. I'm afraid Farsal was spotted entering the building so there is media everywhere upstairs. I'll address them and—"

"My son will attend this conference as well," Farsal said. "I have a statement I want him to read."

"I should be with you," Kemel said to his father. "You need an arbiter to the next life...just in case." Kemel's face tightened at the last sentence.

Despite having a murderous father, Bokrahm could tell his son loved him. There must be something redeeming in the man.

Farsal handed his son a tablet. "I do not plan on dying before you return from reading my statement."

"Don't worry," Bokrahm said putting a hand on Kemel's arm. "I will take good care of your father. I give my word." Kemel looked at Bokrahm's hand on his arm. Bokrahm removed it. "My apologies. I meant no disrespect."

"I'll be back soon," Noam said as he left with a single security guard and young Kemel. The remaining three guards stayed in the room with Bokrahm and his patient.

The analyzer gave the awaited beep. Bokrahm rushed over to see the results.

"I'm afraid you are infected," Bokrahm said. "But I assure you I'll do my best to find a solution."

"I would wish you success," Farsal said. "But that would run contrary to my goals."

"Goals? Are you saying you want to die?" Bokrahm looked at the guards wondering if he should be more concerned.

"I am going to die. No one has survived this illness. I *want* to die while in your care."

A barb of bitterness rose in Bokrahm's heart. This was the man responsible for his Apa's death, along with so many others. Even facing death, he had no remorse.

"I see. I am to be your final piece of propaganda."

Farsal smiled.

Bokrahm refused to play his game. Instead, he put a hand gently on the chest of his enemy. "I will endeavor to disappoint."

Farsal's smile withered as he swatted the hand away.

Bokrahm called in a lab assistant to draw some more blood. The young man paled when faced with Farsal the Butcher. His hand shook as he took out his hematology kit. Bokrahm put a steadying hand on the young man's shoulder.

"Strevent, right?" Bokrahm asked hoping he remembered the young man's name correctly. There were so many lab assistants in this place.

Strevent nodded.

"He can bring you no harm. You are Nakim. Strong and faithful. Do your duty well.

Strevent stood taller and straightened his shoulders. Bokrahm smiled as the young assistant's hands steadied and he prepped his patient.

"Boo!" Farsal shouted, just as Strevent was about to retrieve some blood. Strevent jumped, but then went right back to his duty.

"You are a good Nakim," Bokrahm told the young man, who smiled at the compliment.

The door to the room slammed open and a livid Noam stormed in followed closely by Kemel.

"So that's your game, is it?" Noam was practically shouting, something Bokrahm had not heard since his days as an intern when he accidentally spilled a tray of urine samples on his instructor. "You plan to die and blame us." He looked at Bokrahm. "His statement said that this would be proof of our treachery. He's coming here a healthy man to help aid in the cure of his people. If he died, the d'Nai would know we are the cause."

"You left out the part about avenging my death," Farsal said. "I hope you read that too, my son."

Kemel nodded.

Noam stormed over and poked a finger into Farsal's chest. "When you first came in here, I looked forward to your death. Now I am going to help my colleague prevent it. What do you need from me, Bokrahm?"

Bokrahm signaled for Noam to join him at the holoscreen. "These are the tests I developed. You take the first two. I'll take the next two."

Kemel lurked by Bokrahm's side as he took some tissue samples and tried a variety of antidotes, asking questions at each step of the process. Bokrahm eyed the young man, impressed by his insightful questions.

"You know," Bokrahm said, "you'd make a fine researcher."

Kemel's eyes briefly lit up at the statement, then just as quickly faded.

"My boy has better things to do with his life," Farsal said. "We d'Nai do not fear death the way you Nakim do. I expect you whimper for your mothers during your final moments."

A notification announced the results of the final antidote

option. Two-tone. Failure. Bokrahm cursed and flung his chair across the room. Now what was left?

"Have you tried killing the parasite itself?" Kemel asked.

Bokrahm nodded. "Yes, it's eaten everything I've sent its way. Let's just say if we could fight off things the way that parasite does, we'd be immortal."

Kemel walked over to his father, who had not spoken in a while. "Do you want to walk for a bit?"

"I'm afraid that is no longer possible. I cannot move my legs."

If Farsal's illness progressed like the others, he'd have two days at best. They needed a miracle.

"I'll be back," Bokrahm said to Noam. "If you think of anything promising, contact me immediately."

Noam grunted from his position hunched over some petri dishes.

Bokrahm had less than two days to find a solution. This would require greater knowledge than he had. He'd make one final plea.

Bokrahm returned to the Ghost Forest and gave a fresh offering. At least this time, there was no explosion when he bent in supplication. He would take that as a positive sign.

"Great Architect, they are your children, too. How do I help them?"

Silence. He waited until his legs started to go numb. Deflated, Bokrahm stood back up. Maybe it was a judgment.

The wind picked up. With a sliver of hope, Bokrahm made his way to one of the rock formations to listen for a word from the dead.

A voice came through the opening, deep and resonant. "Look to yourself."

Look to myself? What does that mean? He waited for more, but the wind had ceased. The voice was gone.

Bokrahm made his way back walking the petitioner's path. *Look to myself.* He repeated the words over and over. An idea formed in his mind. It was insane, but nothing else worked. And, even if it did work the chances of *anyone* agreeing were small.

∾

"I'VE GOT NOTHING," Noam said when Bokrahm returned.

"That's okay. Draw my blood," he said as he checked on Farsal. His pallor had changed. They might not have two days.

Noam tilted his head. "What do you have in mind?"

"Nothing definitive. Just an idea."

Noam shrugged his shoulders and drew the blood. Bokrahm grabbed a specimen dish and put some of Farsal's blood in it. Then he took a pipette and drew some of his own blood from the vial Noam had filled.

"Stop it! You cannot taint your blood like this. It is a sacrilege!"

Though his boss was right about the violation, Bokrahm ignored him and put some drops of his own blood on top of Farsal's. He moved the dish to the scope with a silent prayer.

"Look at this!" Bokrahm shouted. "Noam, come here!"

"I won't touch tainted blood," Noam said.

"I'm not asking you to touch it, just look at the screen."

Noam shuffled his way to the screen keeping as much distance from the blood as possible.

"My blood cells are eating the parasite. We can stop the plague."

∾

BOKRAHM RAN every test possible before contacting The Twelve. He had one shot at this. The inner chamber of The Twelve was simple: a stone table and a podium. The stone table had been carved from the ground out of the mountain that made up the foundation of The Assembly Building. It was meant to represent steadfastness. The table took up most of the space in the center of the room. The Twelve sat around the table, each with a decision orb in front of them.

He bowed in deference. "May I address the assembly?"

He heard the whir of the orbs as each member placed their palm on it to register their decision. All glowed copper. Bokrahm made his way to the podium and inserted the data crystal. A holoscreen showed his report.

"It appears that we are the solution to the d'Nai plague—"

"A plague they accused us of starting," Shandret said. "This is The Great Architect's judgment on them. Who are we to intervene?"

Bokrahm let out a breath to calm himself. Too many nodded in agreement. Their hearts were as hard as the ruling table they sat around. He needed to make them see reason.

"The Great Architect spoke this to me," Bokrahm said. "From the Ghost Forest."

"He told you to taint your blood," Shandret said. "That is heresy."

"Can the Great Architect commit heresy? And, if you'll forgive me for being so bold," Bokrahm said, "may I suggest you go there yourself and ask? If you find I am committing heresy, I will give myself over to banishment.

"How would it work?" Shandret asked.

"It's both simple and delicate. Our blood will kill the parasite. The problem lies with the parasite count. The higher the parasite count, the more Nakim blood will be needed. Our best chances are for those in the early stages of the illness. But if we get could get enough blood, a LOT of blood, we could even save those in later stages.

"And why should we save our butchers?" another of The Twelve asked.

"Because we are Nakim," Bokrahm said.

The Twelve put their hands on the orbs which turned cloudy as they deliberated silently. Bokrahm closed his eyes hoping for them to at least let him try. The orbs went dark.

Shandret stood. "We cannot order anyone to taint their blood."

Bokrahm's heart sank. That was his last hope.

"However," Shandret said, "we will allow you to share your findings. If someone volunteers, we will not intervene."

"Thank you!" Bokrahm bowed in deference. "Thank you so much!" He bowed again before departing. Once outside the chamber, he called Noam and asked him to set up a conference and tell the press to announce a universal address.

BOKRAHM HELD the conference outside the hospital. This would require some of that showmanship his Apa had taught him about, which meant he'd need Farsal the Butcher. Near the podium stood Noam and Kemel, who led his father in a wheelchair.

The surrounding lawn was packed. Rows of chairs were set up. Reporters all had the first few rows. The rest were filled with leaders of the varying castes. Families who arrived fast enough sat on blankets nearby on the lawn. Those who couldn't fit into the area were watching from their homes or in the designated areas with public holoscreens.

Bokrahm explained his findings. As expected, a ripple of anger went through the crowd when he reached the part about mixing their blood. Not even relaying that the idea came from The Great Architect softened the angry looks from the crowd.

"You may wonder why I have Farsal the Butcher here with me?" Bokrahm said.

"Let him die," someone shouted from the crowd.

"That is just what he wants," Bokrahm said. "If he dies, he becomes a martyr, and an all-out war will break out. You think the bombings are bad now? Just wait to see what war does.

"What I need is for as many Nakim as possible to donate some blood. We'll match your blood type with a d'Nai and do a transfusion. This will stop the plague. The sooner we get started the more lives we can save. Anyone willing please follow Dr. Noam Chven."

At first there was silence. Then angry shouts at the suggestion. Some even called for Bokrahm's resignation. He feared if he didn't do something soon, they'd attack him.

Over to the right, Bokrahm spotted Apa's friend Engriel. He smiled as she waved at him. He knew what he had to do.

Bokrahm leaned over to Noam. "Take my blood here. In front of everyone."

"You are determined to be lynched, my friend," Noam said.

"Please, do this for me," Bokrahm said as he tilted his head toward the needle and blood bags. "I knew it might come to this."

Bokrahm returned to the podium. "I will be the first. My blood type matches Farsal's."

Bokrahm sat in a chair, and Noam started taking his blood. He'd hoped the act would spur some volunteers, but the crowd just sat there and watched. At two pints, Bokrahm felt his heart start racing. According to his calculations Farsal would need four pints. More than Bokrahm could provide alone.

"I can take no more, my friend," Noam said. "Any more will kill you."

"Then I die," Bokrahm said simply. He turned to the crowd. "If we let the d'Nai die, then we are no better than those who send bombs into our cities. I am Nakim, strong and faithful. I will do my duty."

The crowd watched in silence as the blood dripped from his veins.

Surprised murmurs grew as Shandret walked up to Bokrahm and put a hand on his shoulder. "Take mine," she said. "I am Nakim."

"Take mine," said another who stood up from the crowd. "I am Nakim."

One by one more people stood up and offered their blood. Noam quickly removed the needle from Bokrahm's arm.

"There is no point," Farsal said. "I will not take your dirty blood, and neither will my people. We will die pure."

"I'll take it," Kemel said.

"You!" Farsal shouted. "You are not even infected."

"My fingers have been numb for the last hour," Kemel said. "I suspect I am."

Every camera swiveled and zoomed in on the conversation between father and son.

That was the first time Bokrahm saw regret in Farsal's face. It only lasted a second, but it was there.

"I forbid it," Farsal said.

Kemel put his forehead on his father's in the d'Nai gesture of respect. "You have served our people in the way you thought best. But you are blinded by your hatred. I have seen something different in the Nakim." He pointed to Bokrahm. "This one was willing to die for you. There is hope for our people."

"I am still the leader," Farsal said. "And I still forbid it."

Bokrahm tried to stand to talk to Farsal himself but was

too weak from the loss of blood. He fell back and Noam caught him.

Kemel walked over, clasped Bokrahm's hand, and helped him up. There were some gasps from the crowd.

Kemel turned to his father. "You are our leader and must be obeyed. But you will be dead soon by your own stubbornness. Then I will be the leader, and anyone among our people who wants to survive will be permitted to do so."

Kemel turned away from his father and put his forehead to Bokrahm's, in a show of respect.

The crowd went silent.

"We will be blood brothers," Bokrahm said. "And bring peace to our people."

INTRODUCTION TO "MEMORY GHOST"

This is second science fiction story about brains in this collection. I'll admit I'm a bit obsessed with science. For this story, I began to wonder what would happen if there were brain grafts the way we donated lungs and kidneys.

5

MEMORY GHOST

L eila didn't realize she was crying until a tear fell onto the paper in her lap. Normally, reading through the "get to know you" essays from her third graders was entertaining. They had no filter. This one worried her.

Sitting by the fireplace reading and snuggling together was a nightly routine for Leila and her husband, Theo. Though the room was dim with dark paneling and brown leather couches—manly décor—Theo called it, the reading lamps that hovered over them made it easy to read. A nightly routine. For Leila, that meant novels or school papers. Theo focused on senate bills and newspapers that aided his work.

She glanced at him. Her hero. Helping to lead the free world while still fiercely loving her. He'd given her everything her heart desired, except one. Children. Everything they'd tried had failed.

Though her arms ached to hold her own child, she contented herself with loving her students. This boy's essay made her ache in a different way.

She could hear Theo humming. A quirk of his which meant he liked what he was reading.

"What's got you so excited? Is it work?"

Theo looked up at her and smiled. "This? No. It's fascinating though. A doctor has found a way to perform brain grafting. Brain grafting! Can you believe that? Do you know how many people this could help?"

"Speaking of helping people, would you mind looking at this?" She held out the essay, still with a fresh tear mark on it.

"Sure," he said, reaching for the paper. "What crazy thing has—" His smile faded. "Have you been crying?"

She pursed her lips. "Just read it and tell me what you think."

As Theo scanned the paper, his eyebrows went up. "I think you should call CPS."

"No! The child isn't being physically hurt. I'd rather try to help the family than rip them apart."

"If the boy is home alone while she's out walking the streets, I'm not sure what kind of help will work," Theo said. "Some people don't have a moral compass."

Leila frowned at him. "*Or* she's in desperate circumstances and doing whatever she can to put food on the table. There's got to be some way to help them without the draconian measures of separating them."

Theo kissed the top of her head. "If my colleagues had a wife who doubled as a conscience, this country would be in much better shape." Theo handed the paper back to her. "I'll look into some programs discreetly tomorrow."

She wrapped her arm through Theo's. "My hero."

He kissed her again. "Don't forget about tomorrow night's fundraising dinner. It's a formal."

"Oh good," Leila said. "I've been wanting an opportunity to wear my Tardis dress. How do you feel about wearing a bow tie?" Leila gave her best Amy Pond impersonation.

Theo laughed. "How about a compromise, nerd girl. You

wear an evening gown...a *real* evening gown to the dinner... then, we can play doctor when we get back."

"Well, at least I have something to look forward to after your stuffy fundraiser."

Theo tried to hide a smile.

"I know that smile," Leila said. "You're up to something. Spill it."

"Sorry, I have a brain grafting article to read. You'll just have to wait until the boring, stuffy dinner to find out what this smile is about."

"Va Va Voom," Theo said as Leila walked into the living room dressed in her Midnight Blue evening gown. "You look beautiful." He held out his arm. "My Lady."

Forty-five minutes later, they made their way into the Waldorf's ballroom, its gold accented moldings lit by crystal chandeliers. Though spacious, the room was packed.

A tap on her shoulder drew her attention. Time to schmooze. Not her favorite activity. Leila planted her politician's wife smile on and turned toward whoever wanted her attention.

She squealed with delight. "Kevin?!" She turned toward her husband. "My surprise?"

Though still as gangly as he had been in third grade, Kevin had thicker, browner hair and his bearing held a confidence she'd always hoped he'd develop. He pushed his wire rimmed glasses up a little further on his nose.

Leila squeezed both of them together in one giant hug. "Look how grown up you are!"

"Apparently, not grown up enough that you didn't recognize me instantly. Do I honestly still look the same as elementary school?"

"Oh hush. I've been keeping up with your academic and professional career since you left my classroom. I knew you'd change the world one day. And now here you are, a famous computer scientist." She hugged him again. "I'm so freaking proud of you!"

While her husband, Theo, slipped away to give as many donors his attention as possible, Leila stole Kevin and found their table.

"Tell me what awesome project you're working on now," Leila said. "I want to know everything, even if I don't understand a word."

Kevin smiled. "Well, it is pretty awesome. I've been working with some neuroscientists on an experimental procedure. They've made great strides in brain grafting but have hit a wall. After reading their research, I approached them with an idea.

Leila smiled. That's why her husband had been reading that article. The sneak. "What does computer programming have to do with brain grafting?"

"Well, here's the cool thing. Keeping the donor brain alive long enough has been a serious block in achieving real results. They have a cerebrospinal fluid that can keep it viable for a few days, but with no brain stem connection, they couldn't even test what was working and what wasn't.

"Without that information there was a greater danger in doing the graft. I've created a computer-generated artificial brain stem that can send the electrical pulses it needs to read and send data, mimicking the human body. We're about to do our first human trials."

Leila put her hand on Kevin's arm, tears in her eyes. "I always knew you'd make a huge difference in this world."

Kevin smiled. "You know, when I'm bogged down on a problem and can't find a solution, I use your *wake-up dance* to get my brain flowing again."

Leila buried her head in her hands. "I can't believe you remember that!" Images of her flapping her arms wildly around while circling her classroom and cackling "wake-up" flashed through her mind.

"Can you imagine if the media got hold of some video of that?" she said. "I can see the headlines now. *Senator's Wife Loses Mind: Thinks She's a Chicken.*"

"Hey, don't knock it. Those sweet moves help usher in my last big breakthrough."

LEILA SNUGGLED against her husband during their drive home. Rain pattered their car as the front end of an incoming storm made its way toward them. Light reflected off the rain-soaked streets. She squeezed her husband's arm wrapped in hers.

"I can't think of a time I've been happier," she said looking up into his handsome face.

He leaned down and kissed her forehead. "And I can't think of a luckier ma—"

Leila saw the headlights before she felt the collision.

Her head slammed into the side window. She felt blood dripping down the side of her face as everything went dark.

HER HEAD THROBBED. Leila opened her eyes to a blinding light. She closed them again into tiny slits. Where was she? Slowly, her eyes adjusted. The room was unfamiliar. To her right an IV pole dripped a solution into her right arm. A hospital. She felt like she'd been hit by a truck. That's when it all came back. They were in the car. The lights. They *were* hit.

Leila groped for the nurse's button in a panic. "Help. Where's my husband? Is he okay?"

A moment later a nurse rushed in. "You're awake. No, don't try to sit up," she said as Leila shifted her position. "Not yet. We want the doctor to look at you first."

The nurse had barely finished her sentence before a doctor rushed in, with her husband right behind him. Though his face was bruised and he had a cast on his arm, he was alive. Leila relaxed just a little.

Theo pushed past the doctor and grabbed her hand. "You are a miracle," he said.

Though smiling hurt, Leila welcomed the pain. Her husband was safe. More doctors started filing into the room, which seemed a bit like overkill to her. Was the extra attention because of her husband's position?

"Okay you two love birds," the first doctor said, gently moving her husband out of the way and making room for the other staff. "I need to see my patient. There are a lot of tests to be done." He looked at Leila. "How much do you remember?"

"Of the accident? Mostly headlights and pain."

He smiled. "That's fantastic! Well, not the headlights and pain. Your memory." Some of the other doctors clapped. They were celebrating.

"I don't understand. Why is that so exciting?"

"Because, Mrs. Winthrope," the doctor said. "You are our very first human brain grafting patient and you appear to still have your memories."

Leila's heartrate skyrocketed, which set off alarm bells on the monitor she'd been hooked up to. She had someone *else's* brain in hers? Whose? Where they good? Would it change her? Leila's breathing grew rapid. She grabbed her chest.

The doctor looked at one of the nurses. "Get me 3 mg of lorazepam."

Before Leila could protest, she was falling asleep.

∽

LEILA WALKED NUMBLY to the funeral parlor. Half the room was filled. Only half? He deserved more than that. A simple coffin lay at the front of the room. She could barely will her legs to continue. Leila looked at the unfamiliar faces in the room.

"This is wrong. My husband is alive. He survived the accident." They looked at her with pity.

She made her way to the coffin, legs trembling, then looked down. It wasn't him. It wasn't her husband. But she knew this man and loved him. Didn't she?

As Leila wrenched herself awake, the sky outside her window had turned ink black. They must have kept her sedated for most of the day. What a disturbing dream. Leila stretched her hand and searched for the call button but didn't need it. Both the doc and her husband were dozing off in nearby chairs.

Her tongue stuck to the top of her mouth and throat felt dry and scratchy. She tried to work up some moisture and swallow so she could talk. Through the pain, all she managed was a hoarse, "Theo."

Both men woke immediately and rushed to her bedside.

"I owe you an apology," the doc said. "It was bad form to drop that information on you the way I did."

She lay there for a moment in silence trying to recall what information they'd dropped on her. When she did, a wave of nausea rose in her stomach. She choked it down and said nothing. The last thing she wanted was them sedating her again.

"We should have broken the news to you more gently," Theo said gently wrapping his hand around hers.

She relaxed with his familiar touch. That's what she needed to focus on. Her husband would never let them do anything bad to her. For him to allow this...

"I don't understand. Why did I need a brain graft?"

The doctor spoke first. "You sustained severe head injuries. Without getting too graphic, the trauma to your skull caused an opening, which allowed glass and other debris to get to your brain. You were in a coma for a while, and then your brain started shutting down. You were dying and there was little we could do. That's when your husband suggested we try the brain graft."

"It was a long shot," Theo said. "But I couldn't stand by and let you die."

Leila nodded. That was her husband alright. Find a solution.

"I couldn't believe we received approval," the doc added. "Your husband has some good connections. Even then, I warned him, that finding a donor in time would take a miracle, and there were no guarantees."

"I guess the miracle happened," Leila said. "I'm sorry, doc. I don't know your name."

"Dr. Raff."

"I don't understand, Dr. Raff," Leila said. "It's my thoughts. There's nothing different. Shouldn't there be something of other person?"

"It's a bit complicated," Doc said. "I'm happy to go over all of it with you, but right now I think you need rest. I just wanted to make sure I was here when you woke up to apologize. I'll be in first thing in the morning."

Leila nodded. There was little chance she'd fall asleep with everything she needed to process, but she'd at least try.

Theo leaned over and kissed her. "I'm sure they'd let me stay if you'd like. I don't have anything until a press conference tomorrow."

"No, you get some rest in a real bed." She squeezed his hand and pulled him down for one more kiss. "But maybe come see me before the press conference?"

"With bells on."

LEILA PUSHED a stroller through the park. The peal of children's laughter and joyous screams rang all around her. She leaned down and rubbed the back of her finger on the chubby cheek of her baby in his stroller. His bright eyes looked up at her with complete trust. A tiny smile edged its way across his face. She started crying for no reason.

"Are you okay?"

The voice sounded distant.

Leila felt a gentle shake.

"Mrs. Winthrope? Are you okay?"

Leila woke to see a young woman standing near her bed. She wore scrubs. "I'm here to get your vitals, but you were crying in your sleep. Do I need to get the nurse?"

She was in a hospital. Not a park. She didn't have a baby. The last thought felt worse than the first.

"No need for a nurse. I was just dreaming."

"You should probably tell the doctor you're having bad dreams. He's instructed all of us he wants to know everything, no matter how insignificant."

Leila shook her head. "It wasn't a bad dream. It was a good one."

The young Nurse Assistant looked at her puzzled. "I still think you should tell Dr. Raff."

Leila nodded then held out her arm for the blood pressure cuff. "I will."

THE NEXT MORNING, Dr. Raff along with his team gave her the all-clear. This meant she could be disconnected from enough wires to get out of bed and even shower, as long as she used the waterproof sheeting they provided for her head while it was healing.

A shower! She looked forward to that more than anything. She'd never felt so sticky in her life. Maybe it would help her forget the baby. Her baby...that she'd never had. It seemed so real.

As the water flowed over her aching muscles, Leila gave a contented sigh. It felt so good to be clean. Her body grew tired sooner than she wanted. Reluctantly, she wrapped herself in a towel and stepped out of the shower.

She'd not had the courage to look at herself before getting in, but couldn't put it off forever. Best to rip the Band-Aid off quickly. She grabbed a clean cloth and wiped the moisture from the mirror.

Leila gasped. The face was wrong.

It wasn't damaged from the accident. It was whole. No bandages. The brown hair wasn't hers. Everything was different. She reached up and touched her face. The reflection followed suit. It felt like her, but another woman faced her in the mirror. Leila reached up to her head. She could feel the bandages that weren't in the mirror.

"Who are you?!" Leila shouted. She stepped back and squeezed her eyes shut. When she opened them, the reflection had changed once again. It was her face. Sort of. The bruising was disturbing and there were the bandages and sheeting on her head, but at least it was her.

She squeezed her eyes shut once more, no longer trusting her own senses. Taking a deep breath, she opened them again. Still her.

The remainder of the day was spent going through countless tests. Tests to see if she remembered things. Tests to see what her physical coordination was like. Tests to check her intellect. This must be what her third graders felt like every day.

Leila sighed. Her third graders. She knew they were in good hands with the teacher the school brought in, but she sure missed them.

Once the tests were finally done for the day and they wheeled her back to her room, Leila grabbed the stack of cards the children made for her and read each one of them again for the hundredth time.

Her mind wandered to young Benji. She had not told anyone except her husband about the essay. Their lives have been a whirlwind since the accident, so she didn't blame him for not getting back to her on resources to help the family. In fact, she saw him more on the news lately than in person.

It was funny listening to daily updates about herself every evening. The woman who just wanted to love and teach children and stay out of the limelight was now worldwide news. It was her own fault for marrying a politician. But she loved his ferocious passion and ideals.

The door opened and her hero walked in. "Hello, Love," Theo said. "How are you feeling?"

She reached for his hand. "Well, according to the 6 o'clock news, I am getting stronger every day."

He smiled briefly. "This is your worst nightmare, isn't it?"

"My worst nightmare would have been waking in a hospital to find you were gone." She squeezed his hand. "I'd be on the news every day of my life if it means getting to spend that life with you."

He sat down in the chair beside her bed and lowered the guard rail so he could put a hand on her leg.

"Well, I'm glad to hear you say that because the hospital is hoping you will do a press conference with me."

Leila muscles tightened. Her? In front of all those cameras?

Theo rubbed her leg. "I know, but the world is obsessed with you at the moment. Hundreds of letters pour into my office every day wishing you well and offering you prayers, most with pictures children have drawn for you."

That made her smile.

"You know, there are kids in every state learning more about the brain because of you." He clapped his hands together. "I know. Why don't you look at the press conference as a virtual field trip for the children of the world."

Leila let out a small laugh. "Man, you really know how to talk me into something. It's like you're a smooth-talking politician or something." She shook her head and smiled. "Fine, virtual field trip it is, but tell the doc he'd better have something educational for the kids."

Theo leaned over and kissed her again. Then, he reached into his briefcase and pulled out her favorite chocolates. "For the brave teacher."

"You are my favorite husband," Leila said as she tore into the chocolate.

"I hope your only one!"

Leila smiled impishly while savoring her treat.

DR. RAFF AND MISSY, one of her nurses, came in the next morning rolling a stainless-steel cart in front of them with a giant yellow box on it. The words "Brain Box" painted in bold blue letters on the front.

"As promised. A visual aid for the children," Doc said as he reached her bedside. "Missy made the box. She thought the kids would like it."

He lifted the box off the table with a "Ta-Da!" On the cart sat a pinkish-gray colored oversized model brain. I thought we could go over the sections of the brain for the kids and show them how they use their brain for everything they do. Does it get teacher approval?"

Leila frowned. "It looks very monochromatic."

"True, as our brains are," Doc said. "But the pieces come out. Look." He lifted the front. "This is your pre-frontal cortex." He put it back and grabbed a piece behind it. "And this is your neocortex."

"No, I get that, but do you think someone could distinguish the different sections with some color? Kids do better with clear boundaries."

Dr. Raff looked over at Missy. My patient is doing so well that she's bossing me around. I think we'll call that a success."

Missy smiled and re-covered the model. "I'll make sure it is a very colorful brain for you," she said as she wheeled it out of the room.

"Doc, I was wondering if you could tell me anything about the person who donated their brain to me." Leila said. "Anything at all."

Dr. Raff's lips rolled inward as if locking away his tongue to keep him from saying anything. She let the awkward silence hang in the air as she often did when she needed to force any attempt at an answer from one of her students.

"Sometimes donor families are willing to meet the recipient and you can learn about them that way. Your donor, however, asked for everything to remain anonymous upon organ receipt. I wish there was more I could tell you."

Leila nodded. It was the answer she'd expected, but she couldn't be faulted for trying.

THERE WERE four chairs at the table in front of a sea of reporters and cameras. If it weren't for the fact that every news station promised to put a link on their website to Dr. Raff's lesson on the brain for kids, she would have run hiding to her hospital room.

Her husband squeezed her hand as they walked in, and the room broke into applause. "The whole world loves you."

When she saw Kevin follow behind them, a flood of relief washed over her. Having a former pupil there put her in teacher mode, which gave her confidence. He squeezed her shoulder as he walked past, then grabbed a seat at the far end.

Leila was relieved Dr. Raff let her start with the lesson so the reporters would have to get that B-roll before giving them what they really wanted. She knew reporters enough that once they had the sensational, there was a tendency to slink off in order to beat others to the story. As expected, the moment the educational portion finished, a cacophony of questions rushed at Leila from every reporter in the room.

Her husband lifted up his hand. "Hold on now. Leila has been through a lot and is not used to dealing with you mongrels the way I am."

Leila was relieved they laughed. She didn't want them hostile when asking their questions.

Theo wrapped his hand in hers. "Let's do this with a little more order and compassion. Let's let my wife give her statement, and then you can ask questions."

All eyes (and cameras) turned to Leila. She took a deep breath.

"First, I want to say the science behind all of this is amazing. Each person at this table has contributed to saving my life. Dr. Raff's investment in research as well as his surgical skills are top notch. My husband, who took a chance on an unprecedented procedure in the hope that it would work. And then there is Kevin."

She reached past Dr. Raff and grabbed Kevin's hand. "I knew this young man was brilliant from the first day we met when he was only in third grade. His tenacity and creativity at solving problems is astounding and there is so much more he will contribute to our world. However, there's another person here who is a hero. I don't know who they are. I don't know anything about them, except that they donated their organs. That act saved more lives than mine. If we're going to applaud anyone, I am the last person at this table it should be for."

That caused the room to break into applause again.

Dr. Raff held up a hand. "I'm going to take this fortuitous opportunity to make a shameless plug." He lifted his computer tablet. "If you go to your health portal, there is a box you can check and an electronic signature to become an organ donor." He clicked a few links and held it up to the reporters.

Leila could see the webpage magnified on the monitors in front of them. Her chest started to press in on itself as her heartrate rose. She remembered that page. Had she donated her organs? No. She'd always meant to, but put it off. It was stupid really. She worried that the minute she did, something terrible would happen to her.

Then why does she have this memory. Leila could see her trembling arm checking the box and signing. Except she didn't want to sign, and her arm didn't look right.

Leila started to hyperventilate. Medical staff swarmed in. Reporters scrambled to get the best images of the beloved senator's wife being rushed away. She motioned to Kevin and tried to say she needed to talk to him, but they had an oxygen mask on her before she could get the words out.

Within the hour, the hospital released a statement saying she'd had a panic attack from all the stress. After a flurry of tests, which she passed, they finally left her alone. Leila picked up her phone.

"Kevin, I need to see you."

Less than an hour later he was in her room.

"I think my donor was murdered," Leila said. "I can see it...sort of. It's not clear, but I know it is true as sure as I know you are standing here. I understand how crazy that sounds.

She told him about the dreams she'd had. The face in the mirror. The shaking hand in the memory which sent her into the panic attack. Then the prick of a needle."

Kevin sat silently, absorbing it all in.

"You think I've lost my mind," she said when he didn't respond.

"No, of course not," he said. "I've done a lot of research on brains over the years. The science is still growing but as we understand it now, memory is stored as connections between cells. Your brain graft included a temporal lobe. The hippocampus and amygdala are stored there which do control memory. My system was designed to keep the donor brain alive, but I also used it to help facilitate the neural connections from your temporal lobe. Think of it as a download from your brain then an upload to the donors. That is a major over-simplification, but it is the basic premise. My uploading your connections does not erase the donor's."

"Kevin, I think she was murdered for the parts. Isn't there some kind of black market for stuff like that?"

"Yes, but Dr. Raff wouldn't be involved in that. I've been working with him a while now and he's shown nothing but the highest ethics."

Leila nodded. "Can you at least find out who the donor was?"

Kevin pulled his laptop out of his leather computer bag. "Give me a sec."

His fingers flew over the keyboard. The screen changed almost as fast as he typed. Leila couldn't believe his eyes could process the code flowing across the screen that fast. A nudge of guilt washed over her. Was he hacking? Did she ask a former student to do something illegal? What if he was caught? The last thing she wanted to do was damage his future.

"Here you go. The donor's name is Evie Laymen."

The room started to spin. Leila grabbed the bed rail to keep herself steady.

Kevin reached out and grabbed her. "Are you okay? Do I need to call a nurse?"

"No, don't call anyone. I'm okay."

Kevin didn't look convinced. "Your face lost all its color. I think someone needs to check you out."

"It's not that. It's just..." she looked at Kevin. "I know her."

"A friend?"

"No, a student's mom. A student whose already had enough hardship. I need to find out where he is."

Leila called the sub that had taken over her class while she was in the hospital. Benji was in care, locally. He didn't have any extended family. His mother's death had been ruled a suicide. An insulin overdose.

After hanging up the phone, Leila's stomach turned to acid. She made it to the bathroom just in time to throw up. Evie Laymen did not kill herself. She told Kevin what she'd learned. "I need time to think. Don't say anything about this. Not even to Dr. Raff. Promise me."

Kevin nodded, but didn't look convinced.

"Promise me," she said firmly

"I promise."

She needed to handle this carefully. Her first priority was Benji.

A nurse entered. Dr. Raff asked us to give you something to help you rest tonight. Before she could protest, the nurse had pushed the medicine through her IV. In less than a minute, she was asleep.

SHE AND BENJI strolled down Connecticut Ave. He was younger than she remembered.

"There it is, mom!" he shouted and dashed off.

"Benj! Wait!"

But Benji didn't wait and that wasn't her voice.

Leila knew she was dreaming another memory, but this time she held onto it.

She ran to catch up to Benji who'd made his way into the toy store. He stood a few feet away holding up a giant collection of dinosaurs.

"Can we get it?"

She looked at the price and did some quick calculating. She'd brought in $423 last night, but rent was due, and it was $1300. Yet another way she was letting her son down.

"I'm sorry, pet. It's too much."

His face deflated.

She spotted a bucket that had small plastic dinosaurs in it, about the size of army men. Its sign read $1 each.

Pointing at the bucket, she said, "Reach in there and get one of those."

"You mean it?!"

Benji didn't wait for an answer. He plunged his hand in and pulled out a T-Rex, face beaming. "ROAR!"

Leila woke up. She knew what she had to do.

THEO ARRIVED at 7:30 in the morning. He carried a vase full of daisies and a package from her favorite bookstore. "For my favorite wife."

She smiled at the joke, gave him a quick kiss, then put the gifts on the moveable table by her hospital bed.

"Don't you want to know what book it is??"

"I need to talk to you," she said. "It's important."

"Okay." He moved the table and sat on the bed beside her.

"Do you know that boy and his mom I asked you about? You know, before the accident?"

"Yes," he paused. "I know I should have found some programs to help them, but with the accident—"

"No, that's not it. I just learned from the sub his mother committed suicide." Leila hated lying to her husband. In fact, it was the first time she'd done so, but this needed to be as uncomplicated as possible if she was going to protect Benji.

"That's horrible," he shook his head. "I should have been more proactive."

"You can't blame yourself. There was too much going on." She grabbed his hand and looked deeply into his eyes. "Here's the thing. He had no other family and is in care. We'd talked about adoption after the last IVF failed. I think we need to adopt Benji."

She paused, terrified he'd think it was a terrible idea. Though his face was passive, she knew him too well. His eyes gave away the internal struggle going on in his mind.

"I know they aren't going to release me for another week," she continued. "And only then if I pass all the tests and don't have any more panic attacks, but adoptions take time anyway. If we start now, he'd have a home after I was back and recovered. Please. I can't stand the thought of him in care. Please."

Her husband sighed. "Okay. I'll start the paperwork."

Leila squealed and threw her arms around him.

"Before you get too excited," Theo said. "He can't join us until you are completely well, home, and functioning without any problems. I'm not adding motherhood to your plate before you are not 100%."

"Deal. And I'll work super hard at doing everything Dr. Raff says."

≈

IT WAS a couple of months before they could get the adoption finalized and Leila was cleared. Benji sat on their leather couch playing with his T-rex, which had now lost one of its arms. His curly brown hair bouncing along with the dinosaurs' attack on the couch pillow.

"I have a surprise for you," Leila said as she handed him a package neatly wrapped in blue paper from behind her back."

Benji tore into the package with abandon, then smiled broadly.

"This book has every dinosaur we know about in it," she said. "I thought you could use it for your next report. Do you like it?"

"It's awesome!" Benji put the book aside and wrapped his thin arms around her.

Leila smiled as she watched him flip the pages of his new book excitedly. Benji's hand faltered and he closed the book.

"What's wrong?"

"Do you think my other mommy loved me?"

"Of course she did! In fact, I KNOW she did," Leila said.

"She left me."

"No," Leila wrapped her arm around Benji. "Your mother didn't want to leave you. Something happened to her. I promise you she did everything she could to stay with you and take care of you. Do you understand?"

Benji nodded with his eyes down, but didn't say anything.

"Look at me, Benji." Leila lifted his chin until their eyes met then grabbed his T-Rex. "Do you remember when your mom bought you this?"

He nodded.

"You guys played with it the whole afternoon. You chased her all over the apartment roaring. Do you remember?"

He laughed. "I scared her good. How did you know that?"

"I got to know your mother. Really know her. She loved you with every ounce of her being. In fact, your name was the very last word she ever said. Even though we can't see her, she still lives with us, but in our memories."

"So, she's like a memory ghost?"

"A memory ghost?" Leila thought for a minute. "Yes, and those are the best kind of ghosts because they help us remember love."

Benji smiled.

A jingle of keys at the front door indicated her hubby was home.

"Daddy! Look what mom got me!" Benji ran over to her husband who sat down on the floor with him by the door. Theo patiently listened as Benji told him about the dinosaurs in the book. Leila bent down, kissed him on the head and grabbed his briefcase for him.

That night, before going to sleep, Theo said, "I'm glad we adopted Benji."

She snuggled closer to him. "You're a great dad."

"And my polling numbers have never been higher. Adopting an orphan...every Politician should do it,"

She pounded him with her pillow.

"I'm kidding."

As Leila drifted off to sleep, a new memory came. She embraced them now. It was like getting to raise Benji from the beginning through Evie's memories.

This time, something was wrong. She was scared. She tried to scream. A firm hand wrapped around her head and covered her mouth. It hurt. She felt the prick of a needle go into her arm. She couldn't move. The man laid her down on the bed. The last thing she saw before her eyes closed forever was the face of Senator Winthrope putting away a syringe and walking out the hotel door.

Leila woke with a start, her heart hammering.

INTRODUCTION TO "UNTETHERED"

I had written a story titled "The Problem with Control" that was purchased by Sally Port Magazine (July 2025 issue). I loved the characters so much that I have been toying with the idea of making them into a novel series, which would be sort of a cross between Dr. Who and Supernatural. In thinking about what the series would look like, I decided to play around with the origin of how my two main characters met. This was the result.

6

UNTETHERED

Phineas stood outside the decaying structure of Albright Children's Home, rain dripping down his face. Strands of ivy wound their way up the faded blue exterior and slithered into the home through rotting boards. There were still scorch marks outside the windows on the clapboard and decorative shingles of the upper floors where the fire broke out ten years earlier. The investigators said the cause was undetermined. A fire without an origin. Not even the disasters in his life had a connection to anything. He was untethered. No family. No friends. No purpose. What he wouldn't give to feel like his existence mattered.

Normally Victorian homes were scooped up faster than a government official accepting a bribe, but not this house. Locals considered it cursed. Phineas wondered what it said about him that he kept coming back?

His hoodie stuck to his back. Maybe he should go in this time? That would at least be something new. The neighbors used to call the police on the strange young man staring into the abyss of the children's home. Now they just peeked out their windows in pity.

He told himself that he was trying to remember that night and finally settle what happened once and for all. In his honest moments he recognized the lie. He'd been here the longest, with the same kids. It was the closest he'd ever come to family.

He wouldn't call his time here happy. He spent most of it reading in the nook in the attic, hiding from the bigger boys. They'd find him, of course. One of the things Phineas was most proud of was that he never let them see him cry.

Abigail would always find him after the boys came down laughing. Then she cried so he wouldn't have to. She was one of the few who remembered what it was like to have a mother. Phineas always thought that it was those memories that made her so kind.

Abigail was the best thing about that place. Well, that and his imaginary dragon, Bluebell. The dragon would visit him every day, boldly declaring he was a protector from another world here to train a noble warrior.

A light flashed in one of the upper windows tearing Phineas away from the memory. Someone was in the house. His house. Phineas pulled on the iron gate. His sneakers squelched as they sank into the mud and grass that now dominated the path. Each step closer to the door brought a gooey *schlup*, as the mud clung to his shoes before releasing.

Once inside, the pungent woodsy smell of the rotting boards hit him. He wiped his nose and took the stairs that led to the dormitories. The wood groaned in protest of his steps. When he reached the top, Phineas froze.

Sitting on one of the abandoned metal-framed beds was a knee-high blue dragon. *His* dragon.

"Welcome home, noble warrior," Bluebell said.

Phineas screamed and stumbled backward. The dragon hopped down from the bed, his claws clicking on the wooden floor as he inched toward Phineas.

"I thought your voice would have gotten deeper by now," Bluebell said. "You still scream like a little girl."

"You're not real. I made you up."

Bluebell paused then sighed. "I would say that hurts, but I will allow for a moment of confusion as your brain catches up with reality."

With a slight tremble, Phineas reached toward his old imaginary friend.

"Go ahead. You can touch me," he said.

Phineas sucked in a breath. It was just like he remembered. The scales were both silky and unyielding. As he ran his fingers down Bluebell's side, the colors undulated in blue-black waves. That's it. He'd finally cracked. Did Medicaid cover psychotic breaks?

As a boy, he tried to show him to Abigail a few times, but the surly creature would always change into a cat when she arrived. Abigail would laugh and tell him what a great imagination he had. Then call him "her favorite boy." How he missed that.

"I don't suppose you still—"

"Turn into a cat?" the dragon finished for him. "You might want to stand back."

Phineas complied without hesitation, moving himself back against a wall.

With a small pop followed by bell-like tinkling sounds, the dragon morphed into a smokey gray cat. Glitters of iridescent blue peppered the floor.

Recalling Bluebell's earlier comment about his scream, Phineas kept his dismay to himself. "I don't remember the glitter."

"I do know how to clean up after myself," Bluebell said. "Given the surroundings, I figured it was currently an improvement, but if it makes you feel better..."

With a breath, the glitter disappeared.

"Take me to your residence," the dragon said. "We need to have a talk. Abigail is in danger."

ABIGAIL CHOPPED garlic as butter slowly melted in the pan. Once it started to sizzle, she tossed the spice in. A fire extinguisher stood within arms reach. She always had an extinguisher close—ever since the fire. She still had the shiny scar on her chest.

Though that night was burned into her memory, there was still so much that she didn't understand. She'd hoped as she got older and her knowledge increased, the pieces would make sense. But every time she thought about it there were the same gaps.

She'd just gotten to the third-floor landing. It was late and everyone else was playing in the game room. Technically, the game room was just an empty room with a carpet, but there were two board games in it, so... game room. She'd gone up there to find Phineas. He'd disappeared after dinner. When the older boys did too, she'd worried.

Just as she'd started for the attic stairs a monstrous noise sounded that rattled the house. At the same time, a blinding flash of white light filled the landing. Her chest burned. A strange moving shadow that threw the light away from her. Then the fire. By then, she'd passed out.

Phineas. How she missed that kid, so different from the others. Kind. Thoughtful. Living in his own head. Her favorite boy.

The hair on Abigail's arms stood on end bringing her back to the present. She smiled.

Mama.

The first time her mother came to her, at least in her adult life, was a few months ago. She'd been sleeping then. In fact, she'd thought she was dreaming. It wouldn't have been the first time she'd dreamt of her mother's voice. Her touch. Being held safely in her arms again.

That night, it was just a whisper. *Abigail... Abigail.*

She'd rolled over not wanting to wake up from her dream, but her mother's voice kept calling to her.

Abigail.

She sat up in bed. That's when the voice got louder. Next, the warped shape came, like a faded holographic image having connection problems. It was definitely her mother's shape, though. She'd never forget that.

At first, she thought her mother's ghost had come to her, but the disembodied voice dispelled that idea. It wasn't her mother's ghost. She wasn't even dead. Not in the traditional sense. Just trapped in the atmosphere. And she needed Abigail to bring her back.

Once thunderstorms terrified Abigail. It had been storming the night of the fire. Supposedly that was a good thing. It helped contain the blaze. But it still brought back the memories of that night. The blaze. The panic. The pain.

Now storms meant mama.

She moved the sauté pan off the burner and waited. Soon, if things went as planned, they'd be together again.

THEY WOULD HAVE MADE it to the apartment much faster if the stupid cat had allowed Phineas to carry him, but apparently that, too, was offensive. Even worse, the cat wouldn't explain anything about Abigail because 'Cats don't talk'.

Phineas unlocked the apartment door. "Bluebell, you have to tell me—"

"Let me stop you right there," the dragon said. "I tolerated you calling me Bluebell when you were not much more than a hatchling. You're a man now. No childish names."

"Well then, what do I call you?" Phineas asked as he opened the door.

"My true name is unpronounceable by humans, but I am a dracfelis, so that will do," the dracfelis said as it surveyed the apartment.

The living space was almost bare except for a few piles of books and a giant bean bag chair. Piled next to the chair stood half-eaten cartons of Chinese food.

"This will not do at all," the dracfelis said. With a pop, he morphed into his dragon form again, leaving behind singed gray fur all over the carpet and an acrid smoke smell, like the lingering scent after a firework.

"I thought you knew how to clean up after yourself?" Phineas said when the fur was left all over his floor.

The dracfelis pushed out a claw toward the stack of cartons. "You clearly don't."

Phineas snatched up the mess from the floor and dumped it in the trash.

"We can stay here temporarily, but I am used to much better accommodations," the dracfelis said. "Take a seat."

"Well, unless you're paying the rent, this is where I live."

"For now."

Phineas plopped into his bean bag chair. "How is Abigail in danger?"

"What do you remember about the night of the fire?"

Phineas closed his eyes. Flashes of lights from the emergency vehicles, younger children crying in huddles, water blasting up toward the window, the bigger boys laughing and pointing, his chest tightening when he couldn't find Abigail.

He looked back at the dracfelis. "Not much."

The dragon sat up a little taller. Phineas sensed the animal didn't believe him, though he said nothing.

"Well, that night the fire was started by a lightning strike that wasn't a lightning strike," the dracfelis said.

"That makes no sense."

"That's because you have no frame of reference for me to use. The best I can do is tell you that it was an energy life-form that had tried to inhabit in a body. Instead, it burned Abigail, knocked her unconscious, and rebounded onto the building structure starting a fire."

"Energy life form..." Phineas said. "I'm... I mean I would say that's not real, but I'm currently having a conversation with a mini-dragon, so there's that."

"Well, at least you haven't gone dull-minded, but I strenuously object to the use of mini. I was the tallest in my class."

"Fine, you're practically a giant. Now, finish your story."

"The life forms—Jeongi— have gained quite a bit of knowledge since that night. They can inhabit bodies, but it takes a specific set of circumstances. The particular Jeongi that was at the children's home the night of the fire has focused on Abigail ever since," the dragon said. "When it connected with her it formed a psychic link. Recently, it started visiting her, pretending to be her mother. It will make its move soon, and we have to stop Abigail from cooperating."

"What move?"

"It still needs a body. It could wait until atmospheric conditions are right and grab whatever human is nearby, but because of the link, this one wants Abigail or at least Abigail's body. So, it's having her create the conditions. You need to convince her not to."

"We haven't seen each other in a decade. Social services doled us out to different homes. She probably doesn't even remember me."

"Remembering you isn't going to be the problem. Believing you... well that will be the tricky part. And, if she refuses to, we'll need to be prepared to stop the Jeongi ourselves, which may mean stopping Abigail. We just need to pick up my portable EMP first."

"Your what?"

THE CRACK of thunder sounded in the distance.

"Mama." Abigail's face broke into a huge smile as her mother's form glitched in and out. "I've got everything we need—the propane, the magnesium fire starter, the drone, and I've put together a canister delivery system to attach to it."

Abigail ran out of the kitchen and returned with a box of her materials. "I've tested the delivery system and the drone in strong winds. They will hold. I don't think I'd ever spent that much time in a camping store before in my life. In fact, I think I'd like to go camping one day."

"You have," the voice said. It sounded more like the last vestiges of an echo than a real voice, but Agigail was used to it now. "Don't you remember?"

Abigail tried but came up blank. She moved her head back and forth. "I'm sorry. I don't."

Heat rushed to Abigail's face. She'd forgotten so much. Every time her mother had to remind her of something, she felt guilty. Shouldn't she have treasured every memory with her?

"It's okay, sweetheart," the voice said. Abigail could see a ghostly hand try to reach out for her. She'd already learned that she couldn't feel anything different than a charge in the air that surrounded her mother. Her touch was empty. "You were very young. Only four years old. Her mother chuckled. You left the tent to go to the bathroom and screamed because you thought you saw a bear. It was only a fuzzy blanket I had tied up."

A flash of something big and hairy-looking waving in the

wind found its way to the forefront of Abigail's memory. A feeling of fear, then comfort as her parents ran out to save her. It was coming back to her. She laughed at the restored image. Her father rushing out with his shotgun, glasses sideways on his face. She couldn't wait until she had her mother back in a real body where they could sit and talk together. Where she could feel her mother's arms again.

"Can we use *this* storm?" Abigail asked.

"It's not strong enough," her mother said. "There's a stronger one coming tomorrow. We'll try then. We don't get many chances."

Abigail nodded, disappointed. It was hard waiting to have her mother back. She heard another clap of thunder farther away.

"I must go now sweetheart, but I'll be back soon. And I'll finally be able to hold you again."

Before Abigail could object, her mother faded away with the departing storm.

THE NEXT DAY, Phineas and the dracfelis drove across town toward Abigail's place. The rain started coming down harder. It was getting difficult to see even with his windshield wipers making their rhythmic thud at the highest tempo. An 18-wheeler honked as Phineas drifted out of his lane. He swerved back into what he hoped was the right spot.

Lounging in the passenger seat as a cat, the dracfelis looked up. "Do I need to drive?"

"Sure, your paws should maneuver really well."

"My dragon claws are quite flexible, thank you. Do you want to know what my cat paws are good at?"

Phineas glanced over and saw his claws spread out. "Let's

focus on the road. Can you see the road signs any better than I can?"

"I can see things as if it were daylight."

"Maybe you should drive then."

As they got closer, Phineas found it mildly amusing that he was more nervous about talking to Abigail again than he was about the fact that his imaginary friend was real and there were energy beings that took over people's bodies using lightning.

What if she didn't remember him? Or worse, what if she ended up hating him for interfering? As far as she'd be concerned, Phineas would be taking away her mother.

Abigail helped him survive his childhood. He'd even dreamed of marrying her when he was a boy, even though she was four years older than he was. At the time, that age gap made her exotic in his eyes. An older woman. Now, though, the age difference wouldn't be too bad. He felt heat rise to his face. This was not what he should be thinking about. Abigail needed him.

The night before, he and the dracfelis stayed up late into the night talking about the Jeongi and how to defeat them. Everything he learned sounded like something out of some late night sci-fi rerun. It boiled down to disrupting the electrical signal. His whole world had turned upside down in a matter of hours.

"I still don't understand how it can take over Abigail's body," Phineas said while trying to stay between the faded white lines on the wet road. "I mean it's essentially just energy, right?"

"Your human brains operate from electrical and chemical signals. With the right conditions, the Jeongi can infiltrate those. In the past they used bolt lightning as a portal, but if the host didn't survive, neither did they. Now, they use ball lightning. This way if the subject dies, they can just return to the atmosphere. However, ball lightning is harder to acquire. It requires specific conditions."

They'd driven through the storm and visibility was much better as they pulled up to Abigail's apartment building. His stomach turned a small flip at the thought of her being so close after all these years. It looked like one of those fancy high rises that had income requirements. Abigail must have done much better things with his life than he did. She'd always planned on going to college and wanted to be a scientist like her mom. Maybe she'd succeeded in that.

Phineas scooped up the dracfelis, placed the EMP in his pocket, and walked through the rotating doors of the entrance. A concierge, in a maroon uniform and conical hat, like a 1920s bellboy, sat at a desk watching TV. He looked up when they entered.

"Good evening," the concierge said. "Who are you here to see?"

"Abigail Stevenson."

"May I get your name?" he asked as he picked up a phone.

"Tell her it is Phineas," then after a second, he added, "From the Albright Children's Home." In case she didn't remember him. The concierge gave her the information, including the fact that he had a cat in his arms. Phineas wished he could hear her response.

"Take the elevator to the eighth floor. She's in apartment 802," he said as he pointed to the elevators.

"Thank you."

Her apartment was just down the hall to the right of the elevator. The wine-colored carpet felt too plush for a hallway. Very impractical. Before they reached the apartment, Abigail had already opened the door and had peeked her head out, looking anxious. She was as stunning as ever, with the same fire red hair and freckles across her nose.

"Phineas?" she said. "It really is you!" I almost didn't

believe Carlton when he called up. "I don't have a lot of time, but I couldn't pass up the chance to at least get your contact information and get a peek at my favorite boy."

Phineas smiled broadly when she called him that again.

"There's that smile I loved." Her eyes slid down to the gray cat in his arms. "That looks remarkably like the cat you kept hidden at Albright."

"Oh, yeah. Well, when I saw one that looked like him, I just couldn't resist." Part of him wanted to just tell her the truth, but too much information at once and she'd think he was insane.

Abigail reached out and scratched the dracfelis behind his ears. Phineas was sure the cat would rebuff her, as surly as he was, but the cat leaned into her scratches, purring loudly.

"Oh, he likes me," Abigail said, scooping him into her arms and moving toward her couch. "Come in! But I don't have long."

Her apartment was tidy and welcoming. Fluffy white pillows sat on a large, cushy, sage green couch. Large bookshelves filled with science books and British mysteries lined every wall of the room except where a large television stood on a fireplace mantel. The only thing that didn't have a perfect place was a cardboard box with a small drone sticking slightly out of it.

He took a seat beside her on the couch. "So, did you become the scientist you'd always wanted to be?"

Her smile lit up her face. "I did! I work for Teledyne Pharmaceuticals in their research department. I haven't discovered the cure for any cancers yet or anything, but they let me work on it as long as I produce other revenue making products. I have a cute little biologist for a research assistant, who totally has a crush on me."

Phineas knew how the guy felt.

"Listen, Abigail. I came here for a reason. We need to talk."

A distant rumble of thunder sounded. The storm was catching up to them. He couldn't put this off any longer. Hopefully, Abigail will forgive him for the truth. He thought about what it would be like to think you're finally getting your mother back only to have that snatched away from you.

At the sound of the thunder, Abigail jumped and her eyes moved around the room frantically. "I would love to hear it, but I have to go. Well, *you* have to go. I have something important going on." She ran out of the room and came back with her phone. "Put your contact information in here. We'll get together soon."

Another rumble of thunder sounded, moving closer.

Abigail shoved the cat back in Phineas' arms. "You've got to go." Her voice was tight, almost panicked.

She stood up to show them to the door, but Phineas gently grabbed her arm.

"This is going to sound insane," Phineas said and took a deep breath. "We know why you want us to leave. You're trying to bring back your mother. Please don't do this. It's not really your mother."

Abigail's mouth dropped open. Phineas could see the wheels turning behind her eyes, trying to wrap her head around everything he'd just said, but was too stunned to say anything. The next clap of thunder shook her out of it.

"I don't know how you know about my mother's visits, but you're not going to stop me from helping her come back." Her voice was clipped and sharp. "Leave please."

When he didn't move, she lunged toward the box and pulled out a few things.

Phineas grabbed her arm. "Listen to me Abigail. It's NOT your mother. It's pretending to be your mother and you're in danger."

Her face tightened like she was holding back tears. She frantically attached a canister to the drone. "You're lying. It *is* my mother. She remembers everything about my childhood. Everything. Things I'd never told anyone."

A flash of lightning lit up the distant landscape.

"Get out!" Abigail shouted, her voice desperate.

When they didn't, she grabbed the drone and left the apartment. Phineas ran after her. She took off down the hall and into a stairwell. He chased her up the stairs to the rooftop, hoping the dracfelis had followed behind.

Rain was coming down again. Another flash of lightning and thunderous boom caused Phineas to drop to the ground. He wanted to be anywhere but on a rooftop during a storm. At least the complex took safety seriously. There was a rope ladder attached to the inside ledge of the roof as well as a fire extinguisher and even a portable defibrillator. That meant he had more than one way to get her off this roof if things went badly.

"Leave me alone!"

The hair on Phineas' arms stood up and the air felt charged. Abigail released the drone, steering it toward the oncoming storm.

A warped shape started forming on the roof near Abigail. He couldn't hear what it was saying but saw Abigail nod. A clap of thunder sounded and about three seconds later Abigail fired off the contents of the canister.

The dracfelis ran up behind him and shouted, "The EMP!"

Phineas reached into his pocket, pulled it out, and pressed the button. The drone dropped to the ground, but not before a small explosion rippled through the night sky, giving birth to a shining white orb.

The ball lightening glided toward Abigail, branching tendrils of electricity flickered outward, searching for something. It was looking for Abigail! Phineas dashed over and grabbed her, yanking Abigail away from the orb and toward the door.

"Let go!" Abigail screamed. Then she stomped hard on the arch of his foot. The pain bent Phineas forward as Abigail simultaneously slammed the back of her fist into his nose. He released her out of reflex. She started running toward the edge of the roof taking her closer to the orb.

Phineas ran after her and dove for her leg. He grabbed her ankle causing her to fall, but her leg was slick from the rain and his hand pulled away. The orb was right above her now.

Abigail rolled over and spread out her arms on the ground in a gesture of welcome. Phineas looked around frantically searching for a way to disrupt the Jeongi's electrical signal. The orb was almost to her chest. Phineas grabbed the fire extinguisher attached to the wall and sprayed the orb. As it landed on Abigail's chest, it shattered into pieces.

Clumps of foam clung to Abigail as she wailed in anguish. Phineas felt his own heart break with hers. He gently scooped her up. She didn't fight him anymore. Instead, she held on and sobbed.

Once he got her inside, Phineas placed her gently on the couch and went to look for a towel. When he came back into the living room, she was sitting upright. Her red hair clung to the side of her face. She stood up and yanked the towel. Phineas' heart twisted at the hatred in her eyes.

She tried to wipe the foam from her clothing, then looked at Phineas with loathing. "You killed my mother. Get out before I call the police."

Something broke inside Phineas, but he couldn't leave. He needed her to understand. "That wasn't your mother. You have to believe me."

He reached out his arm, but she smacked it away. "I said get out. Don't ever contact me again."

Phineas turned to the dracfelis. "Please. Show her. I'm begging you."

Abigail looked back and forth between Phineas and the cat. Her face went from anger to concern, as if she worried Phineas needed mental health help.

The cat sighed then morphed into its dragon form. Abigail's eyes went wide and she took a few steps back.

"This is—," Phineas started.

"Your imaginary friend," Abigail said in a whisper.

The dracfelis walked toward her and Phineas noted that Abigail didn't let out a girly scream. He'd better work on that.

"You are a woman of science," the dracfelis said. "You go by observation. Do I look imaginary?"

Abigail shook her head back and forth.

"You've had a lot of unusual things show up in your life lately," the dracefelis said. "You were willing to believe the Jeongi was your mother. I'm asking you to believe me. To believe Phineas. He's never lied to you."

Abigail's lips tightened and he saw some of the resentment come back into her eyes as they flicked toward Phineas. "I believed her *because* of observation. She knew my childhood. Things I'd never told to anyone. She couldn't know that if she was anyone other than my mother. You being some little dragon doesn't mean my mother couldn't have been caught in the atmosphere. If anything, it is more proof that it is possible."

"Again with the little," the dracfelis said, then pointed one of his claws toward the couch. "May we sit?"

Abigail placed the towel on the couch and sat down. "I'm listening."

Phineas sat on the floor. "The Jeongi are—"

"I'd rather hear it from the dragon," Abigail said.

Phineas winced. He didn't blame her, but he wanted to

make this right, or at least easier for her. He wanted her to call him her favorite boy, just one more time.

"The fire at your old children's home," the dracfelis said. "It was caused by the Jeongi. They're energy life forms that want a body. The one pretending to be your mother tried the night of the fire. I stopped it, but not before it touched you."

Abigail's hand went to the shiny scar on her chest. "You were the moving shadow I saw."

"She rebounded from you and the fire started," the dracfelis continued. "But, she'd made a connection to you. That's how she knew your memories and could pretend she was your mother. It was the best way to get you to cooperate."

"So, she... my real mother is—"

"Truly dead," the dracfelis said.

Phineas heard her breath quiver. He rounded on the dracfelis. "You could have put that a little more gently."

"It wouldn't have made it any easier."

"That doesn't mean—"

"No," Abigail, said. "He's right. I was being stupid."

"You weren't being stupid," Phineas said. "You were being human. I'd want it to be my mother, too."

"Listen," Abigail said. "I'm glad you saved me. Really, I am. I just need to be alone right now."

Phineas nodded. "May I contact you to check on you?"

"No."

Her answer gutted him, crushing his hope of a link to his past. Of a friend. Of a family, even if only a fake one. But what did he expect? Did he really think she'd throw her arms around him and call him her hero? Sure, he saved her, but he destroyed her, too.

"I understand." Phineas said. He and the dracefelis walked to the door.

Abigail touched his arm. "When I'm ready, I'll contact you."

"ABIGAIL WILL COME AROUND," the dracfelis said as Phineas drove them back to his apartment. "She just needs time."

Phineas snorted. Even if the dracfelis was right, he found himself feeling hollow. He'd learned the fire's origin. He'd learned there were dragon guardians. He'd learned there were energy beings that tried to inhabit human bodies. The world was suddenly bigger with wonders he'd never imagined, and what? He was just supposed to go back to his apartment and live a meaningless existence? It didn't feel right.

"There are a lot more things out there than Jeongi, aren't there?" Phineas said.

"Absolutely."

"Are more of them good like you or bad like the Jeongi?

"I'd say about a 90/10 mix in favor of hostile."

"Then you need to teach me everything you know," Phineas said. "Someone has to help the people that could get hurt."

"You want a purpose," the dracfelis said. "You've always been that way, even when you were a boy. That's why I chose you."

"Chose me?" Phineas almost laughed.

"Yes, chose you. When you saw me at Albright yesterday, what did I call you?"

Phineas thought back. "Noble warrior." He laughed. "Some warrior. You did see me get beat up by a scrawny girl on that roof."

The dracfelis chuckled and two strands of smoke puffed out of his nostrils. "Yeah, I saw that. We'll work on it. After you're trained up a bit, you'll make a fine protector."

Phineas smiled. He could be useful. Make a difference in the world.

"Before you get too excited, you need to understand what

you're getting into" the dracfelis said. "Most people won't even realize you've helped them. Of those who do, most will hate you for it."

"But I would be helping people," Phineas said. "That's what matters." He liked that idea. "Where do we start?"

"Slow down, cowboy. First, we need a better place to live. I can't train you in that pit you call an apartment. How would you feel about buying the children's home and making it into something to be proud of?"

"Sure," Phineas said. "Let me just withdraw all that imaginary money from my bank account."

"You should leave the sarcasm to me, young warrior. I'm better at it. My financial portfolio is substantial and liquid. I'll have my broker make an offer in your name. The real estate agents are pretty desperate to unload it so it shouldn't put too big a dent in my investments."

Phineas wasn't sure what it said about his first world survival skills if a cat has more money than he did, but right now he didn't care. He could have a home of his own.

His smile faded as he thought about the pain in Abigail's eyes before they left. It wouldn't be quite the same without her.

The dracfelis put a claw gently on his shoulder. "Abigail *will* contact you. I'm sure of it."

"Maybe," Phineas said.

"But don't worry. Until then, I can call you *my* favorite boy."

Phineas laughed. "I think I'd rather wait on Abigail."

ABOUT THE AUTHOR

Annmarie SanSevero grew up in New York City but was transplanted to the south in high school. She writes stories about hope, courage, and resilience in fantasy, science fiction, steampunk, and mystery. She loves exploring the human experience and wants readers to feel like they can do more than survive. They can be world changers.

When she's not writing, Annmarie enjoys learning just about everything (yep, she's a nerd), playing violin, tap dancing, and singing. One day, she wants to go LARPing. You can learn where to find Annmarie's books, anthologies, and short stories on her website: https://asansevero.com/

www.ingramcontent.com/pod-product-compliance
Lightning Source LLC
Chambersburg PA
CBHW070936250626
47159CB00009B/3269